Moist Petals

A Poetic Novel

Moist Petals

SARYU PARIKH

TATE PUBLISHING
AND ENTERPRISES, LLC

Published by Tate Publishing & Enterprises, LLC
127 E. Trade Center Terrace | Mustang, Oklahoma 73064 USA
1.888.361.9473 | www.tatepublishing.com

Tate Publishing is committed to excellence in the publishing industry. The company reflects the philosophy established by the founders, based on Psalm 68:11,
"The Lord gave the word and great was the company of those who published it."

Book design copyright © 2015 by Tate Publishing, LLC. All rights reserved.
Cover design by Gian Philipp Rufin
Interior design by Gram Telen

Published in the United States of America

ISBN: 978-1-68118-906-2
Fiction / Romance / General
15.05.01

Acknowledgments

I count my blessings and acknowledge the gentle and perfect editing help of our daughter Sangita and the expert editing of my friend Dr. Vivian Brown. I appreciate Munibhai, Mridul, Samir, and Neil for their interest.

Creative energy is much-needed oil for our life light to illuminate the path we travel. We cannot direct the wind, but we can adjust the sails. I am thankful for the keen and kind critique of my husband, Dilip, who facilitates and encourages my sail…

I am thankful to the team at Tate Publication for the pleasant experience.

—Saryu

Sprinkles of Love

Misty sweet dreams, come sleep beside me.
The shades of the rainbow, I have yet to see.
My topsy-turvy mind!
Enough of this ploy,
Rest and relish, there are moments to enjoy.

The story of a simple girl, Sumi, begins in a city
in India in the 1940s. The story is told in prose
and verse. Inspiration is what touches your spirit, and
that is why one would embrace something with all her
love, while another would not give a second look.
I share my petals of poems to soothe some hearts.

"... Someone loves me!
I found the joy, none other like this before.
I am dying with these strange sensations,
but I never felt so alive before..."
She was reflecting the true and pure ecstasy,
and time stood by to let their feelings flow.

The tantalizing tunes are gently repeating.
A secret song of love her heart is reciting.
The buds are blooming and the birds are cooing.
The buzz all around hums; he is pursuing!

Contents

Moist Petals

The garden blissfully blooms, and birds
gladly sing, under the love sprinkles of
Mother Nature,
A bud gently opens, feeling free from the
tangles.
Beaming in sunshine, the moist petals smile;
Same as the people blossom in the warmth
of love.

Sumi was sitting in her lab, daydreaming about the marriage prospect. Raju had come, stayed in her town for two days, and gone back yesterday. She liked walking along his side. She liked the touch of his hand when he shook hers. She liked his smiling eyes. Sumi could not find any annoying pinching moment. Well, the purple flowers on a tall tree were swaying with the breeze, and so was she.

Her friend Minu walked in, which brought her back from that fanciful place. Minu and Sumi were college friends and were working on different research projects at the same institution. Sumi used to share her secrets with her—sparingly. Minu had seen Raju when he had come to the lab to pick up

Sumi. At that time, Sumi had to tell Minu a few details about the young visitor. She did not have a clue that Minu would make her life difficult again in the coming weeks.

Her childhood friend Priya was another story. Sumi shared everything with Priya, her lifelong partner in crime and joy. Sumi told Priya all the details about Raju's visit. She was excited. But after her last interlude, her mind would take a long and hard look at any situation. She was wondering why life had to get so complicated! Her gentle heart was still hurting. She had found out who her real friends were.

After all the struggles, she had come to a point where she saw a good future with Raju. She knew her mother's feelings very well. She had seen panic in her mother's eyes at the thought of Sumi going away. But her father had his opinions about Raju, and Sumi had a hard time accepting them…From the childhood, Sumi was taught to treat each individual differently—according to their caste. After all that training, why did she end up falling for the boy from the lower caste? She was expected to follow the rules blindly. Naturally, the elders were upset with her.

Many questions clouded her mind and confused her heart. What would happen? Her older friend Anu could advise her, but she was far away, in Northern India.

She prayed…

Moist Petals

*The dewdrops of your blessings
on the petals of my life,
O God! Give me wisdom,
to Receive, Embrace, and Let go...*

Though Sumi had lived all of her twenty-two years in the same place—a medium-sized city in Gujarat State in India, her adventurous nature had taken her many places. She had also lived in the big city of Vadodara for two years to finish her postgraduation studies. In her small family of four, she had experienced bittersweet and simple pleasures of life.

As a child, Sumi had to learn to adapt to two different families. On one side, she spent a lot of time learning about the simplicity of life from her kindhearted father Mohan, her aunts, and other neighbors.

They kept a close watch on Sumi about upholding the traditions, saying, "This is for your own good."

The school was always in walking distance; in other words, she always had to walk to school. No other choice was offered. When she had some footwear on, she was admired by other children. On the way home, the kids would help themselves to fruit growing on trees if they could stand on each other's shoulders and reach one in a neighbor's yard and devour raw mangos or guavas. They were not afraid of being yelled at, but if their parents were informed...it could become an unpleasant situation.

Sumi's mother, Januma's side of the family was well-educated, cultured, and rich, especially one relative of her mom's who was a proud owner of a dinky car. That was the only car in the area as far as Sumi knew, though her vision covered only a small radius. It was difficult to deal with her wealthy arrogant cousins. Sumi used to manage, but her brother, Shan, often suffered put-downs for being the son of an ordinary school teacher. His gentleness was challenged, and that used to make him feel more nervous. Well, her cousins' childhood confidence, which was propped up by their successful father, was not sustained into their adulthood; and Shan proved his supremacy with his own abilities.

Januma's older brother, mamu, had a very positive influence on Sumi and Shan. He was an administrator in the county school district and a poet. His connection with a great literary circle provided Sumi and Shan a treasure of life. Mamu was blamed for putting unruly ideas in Sumi's head.

She had her cousins nearby to quarrel, but at the same time, they were her circle of strength, a group of playmates, and a solid support system during a vulnerable time in her life. The luring entertainment was to watch the black-and-white movie showed in the playground—a rare and joyous occasion.

The young independent India had moved society toward the modern world, but the loyalty to religious traditions was intact. Sumi's parents, like many others of their generation, were firm followers of discipline and noble principles. They considered themselves quite liberal minded, but the younger generation would come up with more revolutionary ideas, and the unending conflicts would continue.

Society was energized to promote education for women, freedom to work, and their equality to men. The male-dominated congregations were trying their best to keep the monarchy safe. Sumi's generation was rushing forward with a jovial force, like the holy river Ganges was rushing from Gangotri.

> The energetic youth, climbing a peak,
> Marvelous, mystical, wonderful, slick.
> Stages of ages have their own milestones,
> Blessed heart! Cherish each stepping stone.

Would the song of life teach Sumi how to reach the enchanting sentient note? Would she travel in a circle or spin out of the boundaries? She may roam in the blue sky or may gather twigs to build a nest. Life begins at one point in the safe garden, but the butterflies flutter free in the universe. You never know in which color of the rainbow one will be immersed.

Sumi's gentle heart was exposed to many assaults. And some of the open wounds bled for many years. She became more introverted and a keen observer. These situations forced her to learn and prepared her to stay above the muddy water. Human relations took a priority in her life.

She grasped the meaning of nonviolence in hopes of not hurting anyone's feeling. Many times she failed but tried to stay on the path of truth. Like so many other people, Sumi wanted a happy, stable, and fulfilled life. But to have that pleasant pilgrimage, she needed to have her own guiding mantras. Searching her soul, she had partial vision of the flickering light.

My mind is the master, the source of my
happiness.
My hands are the instrument, the source of
my success.
I will play, and try to win,
but if I cannot,
I'll be brave in the course of attempt.

Mirror of Her Mother

Usually, a person's story is not complete without the history connected to his or her parents. Sumi's story cannot be complete without the mirror of her mother's life.

Januma was born and raised in a very small village. She had lost her mother when she was only one year old. It was sad that only after several years did they figure out that the illness was pneumonia. Sumi's grandfather, Bapa, was an herbal doctor and had unsuccessfully treated her grandmother. Modern medical help was not available in the village.

Januma wrote a poem, and in that poem, she explained her childhood story. The little house, her whole world, had two big rooms, kitchen, and a long porch. One room was occupied by the ladies, which included her widowed aunt, Januma, and her two cousin sisters; and the other room, by her widowed father, two brothers, and one cousin. But most of the year, joyful nights were spent on the charpoy cots under the open sky. The end of the hot season would bring the showers, and kids and all had to run inside the house in the middle of the night.

The enclosed front yard was occupied by two cows, worshiped as mothers who provide milk and fuel for the family. Januma would collect the cow dung and then mix with dry grass. The skillful art of making small dung cakes, the pat-pat in beat with the folk songs, was done quite rhythmically. Finally, the round designs were slapped on the wall to dry. And, as her aunt insisted, that chore should be finished before sunrise.

She, as a nine-year-old girl, used to go to fetch water from the river. She would open the big wooden door and step out in the street, which was a well-traveled dirt road. Her dancing anklets and the bangles holding the pot had to rest on the side at times to let herds of goats or cows pass. She would go at her own pace, lagging behind her older cousins, who carried big shiny bronze vessels on their heads.

Januma said, "My cousins would constantly warn, 'You better watch out when the bullock cart comes running toward you.' Good jingles from the bells around the bullock's neck gave us enough time to scurry away."

One day, she had put a little clay pot of water on her head, but the different shapes in the clouds were so attractive she had to look up, and the clay pot fell and shattered. Her aunt scolded her harshly and would not accept the fact that "it was all the clouds' fault!"

The stuffed animals in the playful clouds,
Her eyes in the sky, her feet in the dirt.
The stumble and fall, a broken clay jug,
The dreams ingrained deeper with hurt.

Januma went to a small school with two classrooms and two teachers. One day, when she was in the fourth grade, she decided to stop going. Her auntie tried to convince her to go, but Januma did not change her mind. She was like a happy-go-lucky butterfly that would eat, sleep, play, and perform all the chores she was told to do. The scolding and shoving never bothered her.

When Januma was about thirteen years old, she did not notice her father leaving town, but she definitely noticed when he returned and announced, "My son is engaged in the Mehta family. And other good news, I have agreed to give Januma's hand in the same family. She will soon be married to the boy named Mohan and will go to live with the new family in another village."

Januma knew about the custom. She was like a flower in the garden. She saw other flowers plucked out, but when she was plucked, she was jolted out of her dreamy existence. The girls and the boys did not participate in the selection process. The reason was that these kinds of arrangements were made at very early age. And traditionally, after the marriage ceremony, the bride stays at her in-laws' house only for a day or two. Then she comes back to her parents' house and gets mentally and physically prepared for a year or two. The innocent couple understands about their relationship when they come to the mature age.

Like many others, Indian society attaches a lot of importance to marriage, and ceremonies are very colorful. Celebrations may extend for several days. With time, the laws against underage marriages were effectively implemented. The strict Hindu tradition of only one marriage for a woman gave uncontrollable authority to her husband. A widow, no matter what age, had to live a dreary life.

Januma used to laugh. "Though it sounds comical to the new generation, the blessing always bestowed upon a woman was, 'Long live your husband.'"

The wedding was celebrated, but no one asked Januma how she felt under that silk veil. Her elders were confident. "Why ask? We know what is good for our children."

When Januma was about sixteen years old, she was sent off with lots of gifts and merriment to join her husband. As the custom called for, the girl was expected to go and melt into her in-laws' joint family before she recognizes her own identity. But in her in-laws' household, she always felt out of place. The way society treated women was accepted by others in the village, but to Januma, it was downright insulting. Her dignity and confidence were exceptional, and she demonstrated that through the years.

Her eyes used to get moist remembering how the daughter-in-laws were treated by the elders in the family. Her husband's grandmother was the person in charge. There was one day she specifically remembered. The men of the house were building a structure with the help of the contractors, and Januma and her sister-in-law were handing them the wet clay and cement mixed with water. Januma did not mind hard work…

A neighbor stopped by and asked, "Why don't you hire some laborers to help?"

The grandmother-in-law laughed. "We have laborers right here."

"Oh, yes…How much do you pay?"

"Just food and shelter!" Grandma chuckled. She did not bother to notice the afflicted young faces of the brides…Januma did a lot of growing up in five years and saw her path to the future vividly. Many heart-wrenching experiences made her sad but, at the same time, rebellious. Her soul was awakened by reading good books, which her brother used to send from the city. Traditions and relations tried to crush her spirit, but once she decided to educate herself, no one was able to stop her.

> She saw the light; she heard the call.
> Eager and inspired, awakened soul.

A great encouraging wave for women's education was spreading with the independence movement in India. At eighteen, Januma moved to the city and found a corner in which to live in her brother's family home while Sumi's father continued his job as an elementary school teacher in the village.

Januma was tested and was put into the tenth grade. She finished high school, and against the protest of her father and other elders of the family, she continued on to college. The class contained five girls and was taught by a few professionals and more volunteer tutors.

Sumi's brother, Shan, was born when Januma was in her final year of college, and Sumi came later when her mother became a high school teacher. Years later, Januma would have a third child, another girl.

Januma was the first female college graduate, not only in the two families but also of the two villages. The change in her personality was tremendous. She challenged some traditions, like covering her face with a veil, having to wear a nose ring, or wearing colorful saris as a married woman. Sumi saw her beautiful mother in simple white cotton saris, the positive influence of Mahatma Gandhi era. Sumi saw her mother the happiest when reciting her poetry on the stage, usually the one female poet among a group of men.

Her mother was like a sunflower in Sumi and her brother's lives. Her children were her sun and moon, and she was looking after them wherever they went, but she had her own identity. She had great expectations from her children and would not tolerate any unworthy behavior. Sumi always tried to remember the wisdom of her mother. One day when she was repeating an unkind story to her friend, Januma overheard and told Sumi, "Do not spread poison." Another piece of good advice was, "Do not let anyone control you."

The fearless spirit in Sumi was passed on from her mother, and her advice had illuminated her path.

The butterfly reveled in bittersweet honey;
Which was prized more than money.
In the seasons of drought, she sipped that honey.
She strongly thrived till the sky turned sunny.

Suman…a Flower

The songs of sacrifice and freedom were empowering India. The time was around mid-1940s. Suman was born in a small home, a part of her grandfather and uncle's house. Januma named her little girl Suman, meaning "flower."

Her mother, Januma, described the joy of her arrival was announced by ringing the bells and distributing sweets in the neighborhood…Suman also remembered other stories she had told about her difficult daily routine as a working mother. Januma had very little help and money—so she felt embarrassed to welcome her colleagues or class students into her shabby home.

Little Sumi learned to walk, talk, and run at the big playground in front of their home. Sumi was cared for by a servant while her mother went to work. But she was surrounded by several loving distant relatives and neighbors. In the lap of nature, she wore the ornaments made of tendrils and chased the butterflies. She had to learn to fend for herself—just like a wildflower growing under the shades of the trees.

Sumi was about seven years old when a lady doctor came to her house one evening. The next morning, the chirping birds and happy voices woke her up. The middle door was closed, so she sat there, waiting. The smiling face of her auntie showed up and asked, "You want to come and see your little sister?" Sumi's big eyes were wider when she saw a small creature sleeping next to her mother. Her mother's bed was near the window...Sumi assumed that the baby came through the window from the sky.

Those days, moms did not publicize their pregnancies and kept their big bellies hidden behind draped saris. Sumi carried around the cloud of mystery. From then on, whenever she went to see a new baby, she would notice that the bed was next to a window. When Sumi shared that acquired knowledge, people laughed. She wondered, "What is so funny?"

Her family began to revolve around the baby, and Sumi had to play the role of a responsible big sister. The baby, named Uru, would be in cradle, and someone had to pull the string and sing lullaby often. Nobody had heard about the stroller or crib or the diapers. What? A separate room for the baby? Could be in the fairy tales.

Sumi's parents were stepping up the social ladder. They enjoyed the increasing comforts available to their social status. The electric wires were installed in every room, and with a flip of the switch, the rooms were illuminated...Wow!

How could she forget that day? A small box, called radio, was hand delivered to her house by Thakarbhai, the owner of a small shop. Her mother had made it possible. Sumi and her brother were standing guard as the neighbors, kids, and all came to admire their new singing magic box. Her parents had warned everyone to be gentle turning on the radio or not to touch. The pride of ownership was immeasurable when friends would gather around and listened to the radio at their house.

Her teen years were an awkward age for Sumi. Her insecurity about her looks was played on by her older brother and little sister, who used to tease her to the point of tears. But within the innocence of her simple life, she always remembered one special person who arrived at her house one day with a camera. He was Sumi's cousin's husband from Mumbai.

The excitement of family members dressing up to have pictures taken was very special for Sumi. Both sisters gussied up in similar silk dresses, and pictures were taken of Sumi holding her little sister in her lap or everyone standing in a line. After years, she felt fortunate for that day because that was the only time her family had their pictures taken with little Uru.

After looking at her pictures, she thought, *Aha! I am good-looking. The kids say ugly things to me are stupid.*

Shortly after that, they took a trip to her mother, Januma's village, where Uru was serenely happy. But

Sumi was exasperated by the weird experience of a village wedding. The groom's party was loaded in four bullock carts. Sumi always remembered how she was squeezed between two aunts. "The silly relatives believe that children do not need any space to sit!" She also relished the memories when whole group stopped by the richly flowing river. The men went away on far side so women could have fun in the water. The feel of cool water in the warm afternoon was rejuvenating for everyone, but for Sumi and other kids, it was an enchanting play pool.

When they returned home, the radio was gone!

"Oh! That? I sold it," her father said teasingly. She saw her mother smile, and tears of anger welled up in Sumi's eyes. It was a most shocking news, and she was about to start a huge tantrum.

"Bena, I'm just joking…A house lizard entered from the back side of the radio, so I had to give it to Thakarbhai to fix it."

The little girl did let her father know, "We are not amused."

They say the hardest kind of death is a sudden death. When Sumi's little sister died suddenly at age five, Januma was inconsolable. Uru had a fever, and by the evening, she started to have convulsions. Her doctor–uncle and another pediatrician had just stepped out after examining Uru. They were urgently called back in the house because she had stopped breathing! Sumi saw the ghastly look in their parents'

and brother's eyes as the doctor tried to revive Uru...
and failed.

Sumi saw, for several moments, her mother stared
at her dead little girl with fixed eyes like those of a
statue; then she bent down until her forehead touched
the floor to suppress a squeal. The frozen grief melted
in tears.

The soft yellow petals had held seeds together.
Sumi didn't know that the sunflower shed tears.

> The sun and her smile had faced varied
> weather.
> But the thunder was fierce;
> The sunflower couldn't stop the torrential
> tears.

Eleven-year-old Sumi also cried with the family,
but it did not take long for her to open a treasure
box and adorn herself with shiny gold jewelry. Her
mother looked at her innocent Sumi and smiled. From
a tender age, Sumi showed no emotional tantrums
or childish behavior. She provided a strong support,
which her mourning mother needed desperately,
which was ironic.

The mother–daughter team was unbeatable. When
mother had to go for training or when they had to
move to a new city for her job, their bond was a
source of strength and brightness.

After Uru died, Januma had a gut feeling that
her mother had been reborn as her daughter. She

explained to Sumi, "The sacred soul chose us to be with. Her time was short, but her presence will be here forever now onward."

Feelings do not follow rules or logic.
Intuition, a God-given gift, is elite and
exceptional.
A fortunate few are given a tender heart to
believe.
And some stay dry without.

Naive Teen and Grandpa's Stick

If someone today asked Sumi, "If you were given a boon to become younger, would you wish to become a teenager again?" She would have responded by declining that boon. Those odd feelings intertwined with an insecure existence. She wasn't sure if she had to behave like a child or an adult! And she hated when all the adults around her seemed to have the right to correct that unruly crazy girl! Sumi was learning and experiencing many secrets of life.

Her mom decided to put her in a private middle school. After the first day, Sumi announced her dislikes, "I will not go to that weird school. I don't know anyone, and nobody likes me there." But her mother wanted her to try it for a few days. Sumi had said more than she could understand herself, but for her mother, those excuses were not good enough... So she found a way out.

The next day, Sumi got ready for school with two ponytails tied with pink ribbons, threw the schoolbag on her shoulder, and walked out of the gate. She turned right as long as her mother was watching. Then she turned around, walked a few houses down, and spent five hours socializing and climbing up on mango trees—enjoying the freedom festival.

Those friendly neighbors did not keep her secret and revealed it as soon as Sumi's mother came home from her class. When her mother scolded her about not going to school, Sumi said nothing...Mother Januma had to give in after getting no response from those deaf ears and mute mouth. Sumi rejoined the public school.

Sumi's family continued to live in their uncle's house, which was okay for her father, but it bothered Januma. She was determined to build her own home. Sometimes, she would go to see possible homesites, leaving the children at home. The relatives and neighbors were always ready to see that they were taken care of; what a nice support! Sumi's parents' efforts resulted in a nice home not too far from their favorite playground.

It all seemed so exciting, but before they could move into their new home, Sumi was surprised to see three new guests arriving in the horse carriage. Sumi hardly remembered her tall and handsome UncleJi, Januma's younger brother, from Mumbai. With him were his good-looking wife and pretty little blue-eyed daughter, Risa. They all knew that Risa was the apple of Grandpa's eyes. UncleJi looked just fine until he had to get out of the carriage and could not without help.

UncleJi had paralysis, and he had come to be with his family in their small city. Grandpa was overly worried about his son. In a few days, the doctor advised UncleJi to check into the hospital. Sumi heard her uncle's pleading voice saying, "No, please not the hospital." But he was admitted anyway.

When other elders were busy and Grandpa was at the hospital, Sumi and her cousins were left to entertain each other. Sumi, about two years older than the other two girls, was considered the leader and caretaker of the group. On one unforgettable day, the other cousin Kim started teasing Risa, and little Sumi joined in the fun, which made Risa cry for some time.

In the evening, when grandpa came home, he heard from Risa about the teasing. He was quite upset and frustrated. So when he got hold of his stick and asked, "Where is Sumi?" Sumi ran as fast as she could to the neighbor's house and hid herself in the backyard barn. She heard Grandpa's stick stomping and some words here and there. She could feel the kids and adults watching this free show with a smirk. Then Grandpa returned, and all was quiet, except Sumi's nerves.

Sumi's grandpa taught her a life's lesson with the stomping of his stick.

> Never follow a senseless wild.
> Never mock a helpless child...

Sumi's uncle passed away…Risa was bewildered and crushed without her father. The shadow of the death was dark and scary. The adults forgot to speak, and the children forgot to shout. The snuffles of Grandpa weeping at night made Sumi to hide under the covers. Risa's mother was dressed in the plain white sari. And she neither wore colorful bangles on her wrist nor the bindi on her forehead—traditional attire for a widow. She would cry every time any mourner came by, while Risa helplessly witnessed the heartrending drama. One time, Sumi's mamu ordered the mourners to stop wailing, and the mourners were too stunned to make any sound.

Risa on the swing,
"Papa, push me so high, I can touch the
sky"
The anchor just broke…no papa…no swing

Unknowingly, Sumi assumed the role of a protective sister to Risa. Though she might push her around, but she would not let any other kid harm her. The day came when Sumi had to learn to ride a bike, one of the necessities of a young person. One nice day, her brother volunteered to teach her. Sumi put on her new dress and excitedly went to the playground. In a short time, with a torn dress and bruised ego, off she went blaming everyone else but herself. And the whole scenario was extremely entertaining for giggling little Risa.

Risa was laughing again.

Sumi eventually learned to ride a bike.

Even surrounded by people and with somewhat stable family life, Sumi felt something was missing. She had seen some other kids pampered by their families, moreover, their grandparents. She hardly ever felt that she was the center of her parents' lives. Her rebellious mind used to think, *No matter how much world would change, the boys in the family would remain more important.* The distance was established between two generations, maybe due to the custom where children touch their parents' feet and receive blessings. Sumi did not remember getting a warm hug from her father or exclusive praise from her mother. That's the way it was in her family.

Though it seemed silly as she matured, her one big reason of jealousy was his overachiever skinny older brother, Shan.

"Sumi! Go find your brother. He is never here, as you are, when food is ready." She would stomp her feet, then run, howling his name. Her anger seemed very comical for her family and neighbors, who would hide their laughing faces from her.

That's why Sumi always remembered that night, when her longing heart did get the sweet sprinkles of expressed love from her mom!

Sumi had to finish her last two years of high school in another small city where her mother had been hired as a high school principal. When her final year board exam result came, Sumi was enjoying vacation back home. Her mother came home by the midnight train. Sumi was asleep on the terrace when her mother gently kissed her awake and told her how proud she was of Sumi for ranking number one in her school.

> The happy teenager sleeping on the terrace,
> in the hush of night, Mama came to caress.
> She whispered gentle words,
> "A kiss for my miss. Be always number one,
> Sweetie!
> That's what I wish."

"Science college, here I come!" Sumi moved about on the college campus quite confidently. Sumi sailed through her first year easily. The second year of college was critical because that year's result would admit a student into medical or engineering college.

The second year, when she should have concentrated on her studies, her right brain started working overtime and pushed her to learn the sitar, an enchanting instrument. She used to rush through chemistry lab to reach the sitar class on time. She did not get into medical school by a few points...her first experience of embarrassment in her school career. Every failure made her wiser, but this turned out to be a defining moment for Sumi.

Sumi convinced herself to make the best of the alternate opportunity. A degree in botany or chemistry and maybe a PhD seemed to be her new future path.

Jyoti, her best friend of those two years in college, said, "I cannot believe that I am going to the medical school without you. Whom will I turn to for help?"

Sumi and Jyoti's hearts were interwoven, and Sumi was there for her in several delicate situations. Jyoti looked up to Sumi. They both were bonded with an invisible, unbreakable, and loyal bond. After Jyoti joined the medical school in another city, they were far away from each other, but they kept in touch. Sumi was always available to be a protective consultant for her. After finishing medical school, Jyoti went away for further studies. At that time, they were unaware of the tragedy that was to come.

Some six years had passed. Sumi knew that Jyoti was successfully progressing in Midwest City in the USA...One day, with a strong jolt, the news came: Jyoti was murdered in a random act of cruel violence.

Sumi's heart bled with guilt and pain.

Jyoti's father said, "I feel pain and feel remorse that I could not protect my daughter, but why do you feel guilty, Sumi?"

"Uncle, I can't help it. I had taken the role of a protective friend, and I couldn't do anything for Jyoti." Sumi blamed herself for not working hard enough to get into the medical college and not being with Jyoti wherever she went. This logic did not

make much sense to other people, but desperate Sumi
mourned her friend's atrocious death in her own way.

The bond was broken with a horrible knife,
an irreplaceable loss of a precious life.
A life was closed, and a deep wound was
opened.
It wasn't only one, but many lives were
trodden.
A flower was battered,
and the petals were scattered.

Sumi naively searched for Jyoti's face in crowd
for many years. After a long time, Sumi felt peace
when Jyoti came in her dream and stroked her wound
gently. At that moment, Sumi faced her fear. The
awakening brightened the dark corner of her heart,
and she heard Jyoti saying, "O my soul sister! I am
here, near you."

Independence Day Parade

Sumi's third year of college was filled with a whirlwind of activities. She participated in a group dance festival, went to the state level to play basketball, and was invited to sing on the national radio. She had been a tenacious member of the National Cadet Corp, known as NCC, since her middle school years. The NCC aims to develop character, comradeship, discipline, and the secular outlook promoting the spirit of adventure and ideals of selfless service amongst young citizens.

She had gone through the rigorous training, even learned to handle the rifle. One cool day, she received news beyond her expectations.

That day, she was sitting there on the university lawn with Joya and some other friends. An officer stopped by and said, "Sumi, you are selected as the best cadet from our city."

Her lifelong dream was realized when she was chosen as the best cadet from her city and would attend the twenty-sixth January Independence Day Parade in the capital of India, New Delhi. A big cheer went up, but the question in all eyes was, "What about Joya?"

Her good friend, a more dedicated and promising candidate, was selected as a backup to Sumi. Joya wanted to make sure, so to humor her, Sumi took her bike with her friend Joya riding behind and trudged to the main office to make sure that there was no mistake. Upon confirmation, Joya congratulated Sumi, but her eyes could not hide her disappointment. Sumi knew that their friendship would not be the same anymore.

The day arrived to go for the monthlong adventurous trip. Sumi made the preparations with the minimal resources available to her family. She rushed to catch the train to go to the state capital first. The lady officer, who had played a major role in selecting Sumi, was huffing and puffing because Sumi arrived barely about ten minutes before the train's departure time.

She exclaimed, "Always late! What if you would have missed the train?"

Sumi apologized, but in her mind, she said, *You are wrong on both counts. I am hardly ever late, and I would not have missed this train for the world.*

All the cadets from her state gathered and were trained for one week, and then they proceeded to go to New Delhi.

Nineteen years old, bubbling with joy.
She felt as if the world just started with ahoy.

This was her first journey out of state. She saw young energy all around her, boys and girls getting quite cozy in couples. She was just happy to observe what was going on among those big city kids…

It was early morning when the train pulled into the New Delhi station. The cold air was sharp, but for youngsters, that was exhilarating. The Hindi-speaking Chaiwalas were hiding their faces with warm mufflers, busy handing out the tea. Naturally, New Delhi, the capital of India, is the city of the international glamour. The men dressed in their fine suites and stylish ladies in silk saris and high heels… Sumi thought she had walked into a story land.

The group was taken to the far end of the city where hundreds of tents were prepared for the cadets coming from the every corner of the country. There was a divider between boys' and girls' tents. In every tent, there were six cots, and each one had two military blankets. As soon as Sumi and her group saw the blankets, they put them to good use to warm up their shivering little bodies. The open sky, the aroma from the kitchen and the commotion of many young students—the whole situation was nostalgically melodious for Sumi.

Every morning, the cadets had to get up at 5:30 a.m., neatly made their bunk beds, and be in the uniform to go to the parade route. It was an exciting time, but in every group, there would be someone who needed special attention. In Sumi's tent, that was baby Veena, right in the next bed. Sumi would hear a timid voice in the middle of the night, "Sumi, would you walk with me to the bathroom?" And to come out from under those blankets was sheer torture. Sumi had many stories to tell about that innocent face and her pearly teardrops.

One evening, they had just finished dinner when, in the dark evening calm, Sumi heard her name announced on the loud speaker. She was startled. Her officer accompanied her to the other side of the divider. There was a telegram from her mother.

The telegram said, "How are you?"

Sumi wrote, "Very well," in the reply telegram.

In those days, telephones were not commonly available, and one post card she had written had not reached home. Later, her mother told Sumi that she had had a bad dream, so she had decided to send the telegram!

As soon as Sumi returned to her tent, all the girls had many questions like, "How was the other side? Or did you see anyone special over there?" and Sumi just gave them a mysterious smile. She teased, "Guess who was on call duty? Listen…Sheru! I saw your tall and handsome dream boy, whom you were eyeing yesterday for a long, long time!" Sheru, their group leader, chased after Sumi while the group cheered and laughed.

The Independence Day Parade was a memorable, gorgeous day. All these days, they were preparing to march in a rhythm and harmony. The people were cheering, and cameras were clicking. The walk on the Rajpath was beautifully finished. Sumi wrote in her diary, *My heart was bursting with pride and joy when I marched in front of the flag and the honorable dignitaries.*

The next day, the group was taken by bus from New Delhi to Agra to see one of the seven wonders of the world, the Taj Mahal. The magnificent structure expressed the poetry of love, the timeless language common to all humanity. She felt like a calm lake attracting the singing rivulets to its depth and making them silent. Sumi was not only looking, but her heart was singing the romantic tunes with the white-marbled love symbol. She murmured,

> My heart is throbbing for someone. Why?
> The tease inside just makes me shy.
> When my destiny brings him in front of my
> eyes,
> O Taj! I will bring him to share these vibes.

Sumi returned home to several problems and demands. Her mother had fallen seriously ill when Sumi was in New Delhi. The worst was over, but Sumi had to take care of her mother, Januma, and the household routines. Her herbal doctor grandpa was with them those days and was very frustrated about the modern medical treatment of Januma.

The cold winter air had all the freedom to come and envelop them snuggly. There was no protection more than the little coal-burning stove and closed windows.

By mid-February, heat started to return, and things got back to normal. Sumi had to make up for the missed classes and tests. She got second class in the final exam, which was hard for her to accept. That put Sumi in a somewhat melancholy mood. Her grandfather brought her a colorful jump rope.

Sumi said, "Oh! Grandpa, I am too old for that." She never forgot his kind reply.

He had said, "Dear, you need a reminder to rejuvenate your zeal…Where is my inexorable granddaughter? Now hand me that cup of tea, and make it sweeter with your smile." Sumi gave Grandpa a hug before she served him the tea. Sumi did not use the jump rope, but it gave her a much-needed jump start at that time.

No matter what difficulties she had to face later, the joy of journey and the exposure to the new world were invaluable.

You touch many souls and meet many more.
It is not worthwhile, if no place to come
home.

Away from Home

Sumi did not know the whole poem "Going downhill..." by Wordsworth, but that afternoon she was going, daydreaming, downhill on her little scooter. The road was open, so she kept on going and started to turn at the rotunda park at the four roads junction...Oops! There was gravel, and Sumi could not control her scooter. She fell, and the scooter fell on her. She felt humiliation more than the pain. Some people rushed to help.

"Are you okay?" Sumi heard a familiar voice.

She looked up to see who was helping her, but one face she saw she did not like. His name was Nick, her friend's cousin. Nick had come from a nearby village to attend the college in her town. He used to show up out of nowhere in front of Sumi with some lame excuses. Sumi had ignored him and had been rude to him, but he would not give up! That day, Sumi appreciated his help to get on her scooter again, but she did not say much more than a simple, "Thank you."

Sumi pulled herself together, tightened her lips to ignore her pain, and drove away. She felt burning pain on her right elbow. When Sumi arrived home, some arguments were going on between her parents.

"Why do you have to be on stage to read the poems? I never see any other lady among all those men." Sumi heard her father's agitated voice.

Her mom replied, "I am not doing anything wrong, and you have to trust…"

As soon as they saw Sumi, the arguments stopped, which brought a relief on Sumi's face.

"Oh! There is blood on your arm," and then she was center of the attention.

She always felt suffocated in those situations of discord. Many times, she had shed tears in a corner. The reasons for friction between her father and mother were deep-rooted. Her father had lost his parents when he was very young. He was raised by his uncle with several other siblings. Her father's insecurities were increased by a more educated and higher-earning wife.

Sometimes, Sumi used to get lost in a somewhat amusing scenario. She had noticed that her father was very much admired and respected among his relatives. Sumi imagined that her father would have been better off married to an ordinary, normal woman. He would have received the same admiration in his home too. But with Januma, his orthodox ideas and his insistence to follow the old customs were challenged and used to end up in disagreeable arguments.

At her tender age, Sumi did not understand the psychology or the reasons behind her parents' fights, but she used to feel very sad.

So when the time came for her to leave home, in one way she was happy; On the other hand, she wanted to be there for both of them.

Sumi received her BS degree with honors. The doors were open for her to go to medical school or to go for the master's course. Sumi decided to go to a more reputed university in a big city for her postgraduate study. Her older brother was studying at a top university in the country. The expense was barely covered by her parents. But money was not the main reason for her parents to put up an argument against Sumi's decision.

They said, "The same course is offered in this town. Why do you want to go away?"

Sumi did not have a substantial reason, but stubbornly, she announced that "I made this decision, and I am going to stick with it." Her friend, who was also planning to go to the same place, was shocked by her assertive behavior. But soon Sumi convinced her parents and made them smile.

For the interview, her brother had gone with her, but for the first day of the college year, Sumi got on the bus alone. Her parents were worried to let her go alone, but their presence would be more hindrance than help. Though, they did not feel comfortable to the questions like, "Oh! So she is going alone in an unfamiliar city?" They had to let her go.

Sumi did not know anyone in the city of Vadodara. Her mamu gave her one address of his friend in Vadodara, whose name Sumi had not heard before. Mamu had sent a postcard to him. During the eight-hour journey on the bus, she struck up a conversation with a man who said his sister went to the same school where her mom was a teacher. Now upon arrival in that strange city, she was obviously nervous, so that man offered to go with her and find the home of her uncle's friend.

Sumi was hesitant to get in a taxi with a stranger but did not have many options as it was already evening. The taxi kept on going on the wide roads and far from the city, but finally it stopped at the right address. Sumi went inside to inquire about the hosts. A manservant opened the door and informed that the host couple was out of town and their two sons were suppose to return home later that night.

Now what to do? She froze for a few moments…

She thought, *I have come so far with this stranger. He seems to be good. I hope I am not making a biggest mistake of my life by stepping back into the taxi with him.*

The man assured Sumi that he would take her to a safe place. Sumi kept a calm demeanor but was shaking inside. Her face drained, and her eyes had forgotten to blink. The taxi went back near the university campus, and Sumi was led into a ladies' hostel. That man introduced her to the hostel director and requested a room for Sumi to stay in for a few days until she would get formal hostel admission.

The warden of the hostel assigned Sumi a room. The room had a desk, a chair, and some storage cabinets. She finished whatever food she had brought from home. Like a good daughter, she wrote on a postcard to her parents and mailed it before going to sleep. A metal cot was provided, and students would bring their bedding to make it comfortable. Sumi unfolded her thin towel over the hard metal frame and made a pillow with her clothes. She covered herself with her cotton shawl and fell asleep with a satisfactory smile. She was thrilled to be in a safe place. Sumi did not have words to thank that gentleman.

A fish in the ocean trusted her notion.
Maybe angel of the waves held her safe.

Back home, her mother was beside herself with worry. Four days had gone by, and she had not received any mail from Sumi. She had decided to go to Vadodara to look for her, without any definite plan.

Mohan asked, "But where will you look for her?"

Januma answered, "I don't know. Oh! Why did we listened to her and let her travel alone? I will wait until the afternoon, and if I don't get her letter, I will go."

Her father had an idea. "Let me go and talk to our neighbor. I will be back soon. Please don't cry." And Mohan went quickly to his neighbor's house.

Their neighbor, who worked for the railway, informed Sumi's father that the postal department was on strike for three days, so the bags of mail were at the station's storage room.

The neighbor said, "I will try. Let's see if I can find Sumi's letter in the haystack." To their great relief, the neighbor showed up with Sumi's postcard around one o'clock in the afternoon.

In Vadodara, Sumi secured her admission in the hostel and met the head of the department and two other professors. She got the schedule for the semester and some books. After an adventurous week, she took a return bus home.

Embroiled Emotions

Priya was a delightful part of Sumi's family, and no one had said it, but they wished in their hearts that she would marry Sumi's brother and live happily ever after...But with an unexpected turn of the event, her heart was aching for her best friend Priya. During the summer vacation, out of nowhere, a marriage proposal had come for sweet, beautiful Priya.

She had come running to Sumi's house one hot afternoon and said angrily, "There is one rich lady in our town, whom my family barely knows. You wouldn't believe this... She has come up with this weird idea. She has sent a message like, 'I have chosen Priya for my brother, who will fly in from Mumbai to see her tomorrow.' What do I do?" Priya felt annoyed by that woman's presumptuous proposal. She was a rich high-society lady, and Priya's parents could not say no to her. Priya had not even graduated from the college yet. She was enjoying all the attention she was getting from the college romeos. But Priya's mother was determined to marry her into a rich family, which was her own unfulfilled desire.

Sumi walked back to Priya's house with the thought that they both would talk to her parents.

Her father was not home, and her mother was totally oblivious to Priya's resentment. Instead of listening to the girls, she sort of ordered Sumi to come to their house the next day to help Priya get dressed up for the display.

The next afternoon, Priya picked out a very ordinary sari, and Sumi helped her to wrap it. The young man came with his heavyset, gaudily dressed sister to meet Priya, who was sulking and barely spoke a word to them. Her beautiful face was not adorned with her usual smile, but those newcomers did not know the difference, which Sumi knew.

He seemed like a sober family guy. As he was leaving, the first words that came out of Priya's mouth into my ears were, "He is not good-looking."

The message came. "We like the girl, and let's have a preengagement gathering this coming Sunday."

Priya quivered like a leaf. "Oh no. This can't be happening."

The tears started to roll. Her family thought that this was a good match and the young girl's protest was just a childish tantrum. Priya's eyes were puffed up after shedding many tears. Some casual rituals like the exchange of a silver coin and coconut were performed.

Even after that event, she was in denial for some time, saying, "It is just words of mouth. There is no engagement or anything concrete." But things kept on happening, and Priya was tied with the silk threads and shiny gold bands. In a few days, she accepted the new relations and adjusted to her future plans.

> Her bright, sunny smile had been hazy for a
> while.
> Her eyes were moist with the pain of no
> choice.
> The flower of her dream was afloat in a
> stream.
> But, she had to build a nest and hope for the
> best.

The semester had started, so Sumi returned to Vadodara. She got herself settled in the ladies' hostel. The new city and new residence were more difficult than Sumi's confident self had realized. She wanted her first day in the new department to be perfect. But from the early morning, beginning from bath to breakfast, she had to resolve several problems in the dormitory.

Finally, she was ready to go to the university. The previous day, she had been shown how to go to her department by a student who was not very familiar with the campus. Sumi started walking, and the road seemed unending. When she arrived at her department, other students had chosen their lab partners and were getting supplies with an air of familiarity. She moved around the lab nonstop, because she felt that if she would stop, she might start crying. Luckily, at lunchtime, somebody showed her a shortcut back to the hostel.

One thought kept her going. Priya's wedding was coming up, and Sumi had to go back to her hometown next month to be her maid of honor.

Sumi came to realize the importance of home and family. When she had gone back for Priya's wedding, she was unsure how her parents would receive her. Her mother was sitting on the swing, reading a book when she arrived home.

As soon she saw Sumi, she came running and hugged her tightly and said, "I'm so glad you are here!" Sumi felt warm to the core of her heart, seeing that she had been missed.

The next day, Sumi was helping her mother in the kitchen. The subject of Priya's wedding came up. Mother said, "I know that you are not thrilled about Priya's wedding, but you are her best friend, and she needs you." Unexpectedly, Sumi's eyes welled up with tears. Sumi told her mother this was not what Priya wanted and her parents would not pay any attention to her feelings. But it was also true that Priya would not take any chance of displeasing her parents.

Priya's husband was an only son in a rich family. The gifts for the bride were piled up high. Priya was in a sort of delirium. It seemed as though her one eye was crying and the other one was smiling. The

wedding was finished with all the ritualistic hoopla…
She bid farewell to her family and friends.

Sumi was invited to travel back to the university
town with the bridal party. During the train journey,
Priya was close and cozy with Sumi and kept distance
from the groom's family—no more than a polite yes
or no. "Priya, go and mingle with the relatives," Sumi
whispered to her.

"That's what I will be doing for the rest of my life.
Don't push me away yet." She was trying her best
to be strong among all those people, her new family.

When the time came for Sumi to disembark from
the train, Priya was sobbing hard, but her older sister-
in-law consoled her lovingly. Priya went on to begin
her life journey with about fifteen family members
under one roof. Sumi stood there waving for a while,
closed her empty hand, and turned around to go to
her lonely dorm room…

The suspense was over about the roommate. It
was comforting for Sumi to know that her roommate,
Minu, was from her city. Their paths had not crossed
closely, but they casually knew about each other. It
seemed like they would get along just fine.

It was a special day for Sumi and her roommate to
go to a meeting. The young students from their home
county would come together. Sumi knew students
from all departments would show up.

But she was surprised and shocked to see Nick
as the secretary of the committee. The old wave of

dislike went through her mind. There was a short courteous exchange, but Sumi kept herself busy by meeting new students. As a member of the group, Sumi continued to meet Nick and other students every month. She was surprised to see a change in Nick, and it was possible for her to have reasonably easy conversation with him. Whenever Sumi paid attention to Nick, his face would brighten up... She tried her best to tell others, "He is just a casual friend." But still her friends were teasing Sumi about Nick's subtle worship of her.

She made good friends with two young men. One was Sundar, who was an engineering student, and the younger one Ajay was a smart, good-looking rich young man. Ajay was very friendly, and very soon gave Sumi a respectful title: didi, meaning "older sister."

The college functions, picnics, and hostel special days were sometimes stressful for Sumi. She was dreading that Nick might come up with an invitation before other guys. It used to happen sometimes that Sumi would decline his invitation and later showed up at the same function with someone else's invitation. Nick would say sarcastically, "Good. I saved my money."

Sumi felt very comfortable going places with Ajay, her brotherly loving friend. Ajay went away at the end of the year, and she missed that uncomplicated friendship.

In the middle of the year, Sumi received a letter from Nick. She was puzzled that instead of talking with her, he would send a letter to her!

The letter did not make much sense. *It said, I admire your abilities, but you waste time with the people who do not care much for you. I am here for you. Nick.*

It showed a lot of frustration and could not say the things he wanted to. Sumi crumpled up the paper and left the matter unaddressed.

Sumi was home for holidays. It had been one year since Priya's wedding. She had come back to her mother's home for several weeks. Both friends had lots of things to talk about, but Sumi felt that something was amiss. Sumi was describing her new friends and some peculiar characters she had come across. Sumi noticed that Priya was not listening, so she paused.

Without any reference, Priya said, "I do not want to go back to my in-laws' house." Sumi was stunned.

After awhile, she asked, "But why?"

"Because I am simply bored," she said.

Sumi knew that Priya would not speak of such a serious matter for a simple reason. Sumi just quietly listened as Priya complained. Sumi wanted to find out the real reason for her sad demeanor.

The next evening, Sumi asked Priya to go to their favorite temple on the hill. The cool breeze was swirling around after a rather warm afternoon. The sun was setting gently behind the tall trees. The steps were lighted from top to bottom. The lamps were smiling all around them, and some adults and children were pointing at the setting sun. Sumi noticed the faraway look on Priya's charming face.

"Tell me, what do you do the whole day at your in-laws' house?"

"My day begins quite early, but first thing in the morning, my sweet mother-in-law hands me a hot cup of tea. That sets my routine on the right track." Priya went on telling the fun part like sharing the cooking responsibilities with other ladies and getting dressed up every day to go somewhere with the family. At that moment, she seemed to have forgotten how unhappy she was there and that she did not want to go back!

Sumi looked into her eyes and asked, "Tell me the real trouble, will you?"

Priya's eyes welled up as she said, "I do not enjoy being with him. He is fat and does not want to do anything to improve his health or his appearance..."

"Does he take good care of you?" gently Sumi asked.

Priya replied bitterly, "Bit too much." She continued, "I want some challenge, romance and... much more. And one more thing, they are not as rich as my mother thought."

The return date for Priya was coming nearer. One day, she just blurted out in front of her mother and grandparents, "I will not go back." And looking at her mother, she said, "You made my life miserable." There was a silence and stunned looks...

Her mother said angrily, "We will see about that. Go and get busy in the kitchen."

Priya was lectured about her responsibilities and made to feel guilty about hurting the reputation of both families. They could not see any problem for Priya in her husband's home. Sumi was the only support she could count on. Almost one week had passed, and things were very tense in Priya's family. Sumi was worried about her friend, and if she would not return, there could be a big scandal for Priya.

One day, early in the morning, the decision was made by destiny...Priya found out that she was pregnant. Now that was a no-option situation. The good news was sent, and her mother-in-law came to take her home. The presence of a little soul in her womb changed Priya's world beyond her imagination.

She would tell Sumi later that her embarrassment about her husband's looks and romance were tucked way back in her mind, and the creation of her baby took prominence in her being. How it happened was a puzzle for her.

> An angel came and whispered in my ear,
> From now on I will be near.
> Spread your hands and have no fear;
> Sweet special one soon shall be here.

Love Is a Many-Splendored Thing

Her amazing friendship was initiated a few years back when Sumi was fourteen years old. One evening, she was invited to a sleepover. When the invite was extended, her mother was standing there, and to Sumi's surprise, she said yes...Now Sumi could not find any excuse to say no, so she went.

Four sleeping bags were lined up, and during funny chitchats, she was surprisingly drawn to this person like never before. They hugged each other before falling asleep after midnight. From then on, they became inseparable. Sumi would look for that face in the crowd. They would seek each other's company over anyone else. Sometimes, Sumi would quietly sneak out to meet her friend. She started thinking about that person all the time. Her heart ached from the separation.

Things would have been very complicated had that person been a boy. But this new special friend was a girl named Anu, who had come in summer vacation to her grandmother's house from Delhi. Sumi's feelings for her were pure wholehearted affection, Sumi's first love. This innocent love was full of joy whenever they got a glimpse of each other. They were thrilled to listen to each others' silly tales for hours. They wrote to each other poetic love letters and waited anxiously for the replies.

The experience of the tantalizing love, that deep affectionate friendship came into the teenager's life to open several other circles of love in her lifetime. Sumi was sailing with Anu in the ocean of affection and self-recognition.

> She found herself as a winsome soul.
> She learned the value of give and take.
> The sprinkle of love spreads near and far.
> She is ready to receive what permeate the
> hearts.

The friendship between Anu and Sumi brought another problem for her parents. Anu's older brother, Asim, whenever visiting, would pay special attention to Sumi. When she would go to give him a snack, to her parents' irritation, he would hold Sumi's hand in a playful manner. During summer vacation, the boys and girls would play together for several hours. Those protective eyes of the parents would follow Sumi with dismay.

One evening, Sumi was all set to attend an event at Anu's grandmother's house. Sumi had received her mother's permission. That evening, her father was not feeling well and was resting in the front room. As Sumi was prepared to leave, her father startled her with a question. "So where are you going?" He had realized that she had outing plans. "You are not going anywhere at nighttime."

Sumi said timidly, "But Mom said I could."

Her father was furious. "I don't care. Go back inside." Without saying, she knew the reason behind the refusal…Anu's brother would be there at the event. She obeyed and stayed home—unhappily.

It was summertime and mango season. They all wanted to go to a farm in a nearby village from early morning to late evening. Anu's family knew the owners. Again, Sumi's parents said, "No boys." So Anu, Sumi, and three other girls came up with a plan that would annoy her parents but get them what they wanted.

They said, "Only girls will go." Sumi's parents had to say yes even though they were not thrilled about the idea. Sumi was sure that her mother cursed Anu secretly for putting ideas in their daughter's head.

Before they left in the early morning, Sumi's mother told them to be careful while intently staring at Anu. It was the look of a worried mother that the young girls considered, "So unnecessary and unreasonable!" But Anu shivered from that look. Sumi felt her friend's pain. The trip was fine, and they all came back safe to their nests.

Sumi was floating like a leaf, without any definite direction. It was a happy time when she did not have to make any decisions, while other people were worried about her well-being. At the end of that summer, Sumi was at the railway station, saying good-bye to Anu. Anu said hesitantly, "I will not forget the day we went to the farm. Please tell your mom not to look at anyone like that."

Subsequently, Anu, Asim, and other friends spent several hot summer afternoons together in Sumi's home. As a college student, Sumi pleasantly flaunted the fact that someone so sophisticated was her friend. Sumi was completely thrilled when she received Asim's three-page letter in Vadodara.

Asim had described a girl very much like Sumi and had written to her to help him find one for him. Sumi laughed out loud. She had thought about the possibilities of falling in love with this guy and spending rest of her life with him. But she had concluded that she would not fit into his lifestyle. In reply to the letter, she had given Asim her assurance that if she found a girl like this, she would let him know…Sumi was quite amused with this matter. She had no regrets about letting this opportunity for marriage pass.

Sumi was a witness when her friend Anu fell in love with a young man and got married. Even though it was an arranged marriage, Anu was heartily committed to her husband and his family. Married life brings joy, but there is no guarantee it will stay that way forever. Sumi observed in her young life that relationships were very fragile.

One sutra she used to repeat was, "I will not be totally dependent on anyone. I will be happy and

make others happy, as the joy comes from within."
Sumi did not know when such wisdom came to her!

It had been about four months since Anu's wedding.
She and her husband had settled in the northern part
of India in the Kullu Valley, known in the ancient
Hindu scriptures as Kulanthapitha, or "End of the
Habitable World." The geography of the state seemed
very fascinating to Sumi. Mostly a hilly terrain, the
valley was a pleasant hill station to be visited during
the summer months.

Upon receiving a warm invitation from Anu, Sumi
couldn't wait to visit her dear friend in that dreamy
place. At the end of the year, her brother had come
home with some money he had saved from his
scholarship fund. Sumi's ticket was purchased with
the kind consent of her family, and she was sent off
to Kullu on a train. It was a twenty-four-hour journey
via Delhi. After several hours on the train, she got on
a bus.

The bus started to go up the hill on a narrow single-
lane road. For the teenager, it was very easy to slip
into her dream world. She was not worried about the
bumpy condition of the roads. On the way up, she
enjoyed the fresh oranges and apples, the freshest
she had ever seen. The beautiful hills were covered
with green and multicolored plants perfectly lined
by Mother Nature. Sumi did not want to close her
eyes for even a few minutes, and miss any part of
the scenery.

As the bus entered the region, she thought about the description she had read last week: "The majestic Kullu Valley is cradled by the Pir Panjal to the north, the Parvati Range to the east, and the Barabhangal Range to the west. This is Himachal at its most idyllic state, with roaring rivers, pretty mountain villages, orchards, terraced fields, thick pine forests, and snow-flecked ridges."

She was mesmerized by the view, and she forgot that she was surrounded by the people on the bus. She was all alone communicating with nature through her eyes to her soul. She experienced joy as never before.

The bus finally slowed down and came to a stop in the twilight shadows near a small building. Sumi saw Anu's smiling face through the glass window. She ran from the bus and hugged her friend. They wiped the tears and then quietly collected Sumi's bag and got into a waiting car. The conversation was nonstop till they got to Anu's dream home.

In a few minutes, Anu's husband, RK, arrived. The remainder of the evening was infused with formal politeness…That night Sumi thought, *I hope RK is not uncomfortable with my arrival. He seems aloof and quiet.*

The next morning in Kullu was slightly cooler than the winters in Sumi's hometown. The bright sunny sky reflected incandescent light all over the hills. And the frolicsome rays were coming to touch her through the glass window. The small huts on the different levels of the mountains surrounded the valley.

Anu's home had a beautiful garden and was very inviting. Sumi freshened up and went to sit in the garden. Anu came out, holding a tray with three cups of tea.

"Just before you came, the white flowers were singing in harmony with the pink roses," Sumi said

Anu smiled and replied, "And only a silly girl can hear them."

RK joined the group, and after about half an hour of pleasant conversation, he got up to go somewhere. As he was leaving, he said, "I will be gone for several hours. And sorry, I have to take the car."

"That suits me just fine. I don't need to go anywhere," Sumi said. A happy look was exchanged between two friends. After he left, Sumi looked at Anu with a question in her eyes, "Where is he going?"

"He takes off like this often. I have quit asking anymore." They both got busy, happily talking and cooking.

"What would you like to see?" Anu asked Sumi. Sumi expressed interest in Manali.

Anu gave her a pamphlet that said, "Manali, at the northern end of the Kullu Valley, is a hill station situated at a height of 6,398 feet in the Himalayas. Situated on the Beas River (Vyaas in Hindi) and near its source, it is a popular tourist spot in summer and a magical snow-covered place in winter. A staging point for a number of treks and Hampta Pass Trek, it is one of the most famous trekking trails in the Manali region."

"Oh, yes, about three years ago, a girl I know went to the tracking camp at Manali," Sumi said.

"We have to visit Rohtang Pass, which is the main attraction near Manali, and on the way, we will also see beautiful Rahalla Falls and the Rozy Falls, which look amazing between the high hills," Anu said.

On Sunday, they hired a taxi, and both the girls along with RK were on their way to Manali. One more surprise was presented when they were taken to the Kalath Hot Water Springs, around 6.5 kilometers downstream from Manali, where natural sulfurous water flows from the bowels of the earth. In the late afternoon, they sat by the river. Nobody wanted to talk and disturb the calm and serene surroundings coupled with the sound of the Beas River; it was a very peaceful experience.

Returning home, Sumi said, "It was a great trip for me. Thank you so much for taking me there."

"So was it for us," RK replied. Anu nodded her head with a smile on her face.

One afternoon, Sumi found their wedding album and started to look at it with Anu. Sumi had not attended her wedding. She had pleaded with her parents to let her go, but they had refused as the college classes had just started. Sumi had to comply without much fuss. She was very sad for having been so far away on that special day. While turning the pages, Sumi noticed RK's widowed father and two unmarried older sisters. The family seemed nontraditional.

When Sumi pointed that out, Anu said, "You are right. The warmth and closeness is missing in this family. Everyone travels on his or her own trail, and they do not mingle often. You must have noticed how uninterested RK seems when we talk about our families."

"Tell me how your life is here, because I see something off here," Sumi asked her gently.

A cloud of gloom came over her face. "I am getting used to this loneliness. I am sure I will find some good friends here. I feel that I need more time to truly know my spouse."

Soon, Sumi's stay was over, and on the day she was to leave, Anu prepared a very special meal and filled her bag with gifts. Anu told Sumi with tears in her eyes, "Your visit was like a sweet interlude, which will help me to survive the next three months till I go to visit my family...And don't worry, I will be fine."

I climbed one step in the social world,
held his hand and came so far.
My heart and mind in a whirling race,
wish to see a familiar face.
Here is a big beautiful cage;
a lonesome dove, alone I pace.

Dream and Drama

Sumi was thinking about Anu all the way on the return bus ride from Kullu Valley. She had had a wonderful time with her friend, but she was a little concerned about her friend adjusting to her new life.

Anu was alone for long hours, and, moreover, RK was not doing anything special to make her happy.

Sumi hoped that Anu would think about what she had told her: "Life is like a flower vase. We have to keep arranging new flowers through the years so, at the end, it will look like a perfect bouquet. So far, I see the pretty flowers around you. Do you remember your father had a dream for you that you would be a top officer? What was that?"

"An income tax officer," Anu had replied enthusiastically. The reply was followed with the giggles, because as teenagers they considered it as a weird idea from her old man.

"At the present time, it seems just perfect to pick one more flower and put it in your vase!" Sumi had said. Sumi was sure that the wheels would be positively turning in Anu's head around that idea...

Sumi came home very excited, and she plunged herself into preparations to go back to the university and finish her final year of postgraduate work. Again that year in the dormitory, her roommate was Minu. Sumi tried to focus on her studies, but Minu had different plans. Minu often brought up Sundar's name in the conversation. Once in a while, they all would go on a picnic or see a movie together. Sumi liked Sundar, and she noticed that Minu made sure that they both would be seated next to each other. Sumi thought that she was being a good friend. Sumi unknowingly started to daydream about Sundar.

One day, just before the midterm, Minu told Sumi, "Hey, I think Sundar really likes you."

"Did he tell you this?" Sumi asked.

"Oh! I am sure he likes you. Sunder and Nick have invited us one evening to their apartment," Minu replied. Sumi was completely lost in her thoughts of Sundar. She couldn't wait to go to his place. But one thing was puzzling her. "Why had Sundar not asked her directly, and why did Minu have a peculiar smile on her face!" She was too excited to think more about such silly things.

It was a dark winter evening. Minu and Sumi arrived at the boys' apartment. They had cleaned up their place and seemed happy to welcome the girls. Sumi was dreamily moving around, feeling Sundar's attention on her. Sumi had selected a small gift, a delicately carved ivory bookmark, after investing significant time and money. When she gave it to

Sundar, a surprised look came over his face. But he accepted the gift.

In about fifteen minutes, Minu asked Nick to walk with her to a nearby store to pick up something. After they left, Sundar came and sat next to Sumi.

"I am so glad that you want to be my special friend. Minu told me that you like me," he said.

Sumi was deliriously happy. This was the first time she was sitting next to a handsome guy alone. She was half listening to what Sundar was saying. She heard his words like the poetry recited through his magical voice. She was already in the future, flying with the golden wings.

Without any hesitation, she let her hand slip into his and felt the thrill of the gentle squeeze of his big soft hand. She was about to lean on his shoulder when the door suddenly opened.

Nick entered the room with brisk steps, slowly followed by Minu. Sumi was annoyed by this intrusion. *Nick is here to disrupt a lovely moment*, she thought. Sumi and Sundar positioned themselves, leaving some distance between them.

Nick came and sat in the chair nearest Sumi. He looked at Minu and motioned her to sit across him.

"What now? Why do you look so serious?" Sumi impatiently asked.

"Ask your friend. She will explain," Nick replied.

"You know how Nick is. He cannot see you with another guy. Unnecessarily, he is rattled," Minu said.

"Nick! I trust Minu and Sundar, so please leave me alone," Sumi said sternly.

Nick looked at Minu, but she just sat there, determined not to say anything more. "Okay, I will tell you why you are here. First of all, we did not invite you. Minu suggested that you two would like to stop by," Nick said.

Sumi thought that was not so bad. Minu had just wanted to help her to be close to Sundar. She even thought of thanking her later. Seeing Sumi's expression, Nick was more agitated and continued.

"When Minu took me away from here, she told me about her intentions. She told me laughingly that Sumi is so naïve. Actually, I wanted to spend some time with you. So I lured Sumi to Sundar, which was very easy since she is crazy about him.'"

"Yes, Sundar and I like each other. Why are you making such a big deal about it?" Sumi said.

"I'll tell you reason. You see that girl's picture in the corner? That is Sundar's fiancé," Nick said angrily. Sumi was shocked to hear that.

She looked straight into Minu's eyes and asked, "Minu, did you know about this?"

"No, maybe..." Minu mumbled.

Before she could finish her sentence, Sundar cut in, saying, "Enough of your lies, Minu. She's known about my engagement for the last two months. She told me that you knew about this as well and still wanted to be my friend."

Sumi got up from the sofa as if it was on fire. Her face turned red, and her glaring eyes were holding back the tears.

She spoke with a controlled voice, "Minu has presented me as an unscrupulous person. She played carelessly with my emotions and has embarrassed me. Well, friend! I will never forget this lesson." Minu was so sweet and subtle that Sumi failed to realize that she was being pushed toward a big fall...

As Sumi walked out of the apartment, Nick came running after her. Without a word, he stood by her and beckoned a taxi for her. Nick held the door open after Sumi settled in, with the thought of accompanying her! "No, thanks," she said without looking up.

She had been thinking about this one person, Sundar, for the past several months. This rude awakening was too much to handle alone for that night. But back in her lonely room, she changed her clothes, turned off the light, and went to bed. When she heard Minu come in, she pulled the blanket over her head and lay motionless, with quiet tears rolling down her face.

Sumi did not know when she fell asleep, but she was awakened with a start. Even though it was around four o'clock in the morning, she got up and went to her desk. She started to write in her diary.

My so-called friend has betrayed me. She has harshly fooled me. My thoughts about the incident bring disturbance to my mind.

*There is chaos surrounding my heart. But
they cannot do anything to me. I started
to fly too high, too soon. I have to give
myself some time to mend my broken
wings, and I will be fine.*

She closed her diary and went back to sleep. Sumi
was so upset with Minu she wanted to move out
of her room. But it would have been impossible to
find anyone to switch rooms with in the middle of
the year.

The next day whenever Minu was near, Sumi
ignored her. But she could not stop Sundar's face
surfacing in front of her mind's eyes. His magical
voice had turned into a noisy clamor…In the evening
when she returned from her class, she was relieved to
enter the empty room.

At around six thirty, she heard her name being
called from the visiting room. From the third floor,
she asked the guard who the visitor was, and he
replied, "Nick."

Sumi was not ready to talk to anyone, especially
Nick. So she told the guard, "Tell him I am not here."

The following Saturday, there was a funfair at the
fine arts college. Sumi went with some friends and
was enjoying the festivities. Among the crowd, she
noticed Nick. Sumi waved and smiled at him, but
he just angrily glared at her. Sumi was confused and
made her way toward him.

"Hello, what is the reason for this angry look?" Sumi said.

"Now is not the time to talk about it, and I don't want to say anything that I might regret later," Nick replied. He started to walk away, but Sumi followed him and caught up with him, away from the crowd.

"Tell me. Why are you so angry?" Sumi pleaded.

"Do you remember last Monday evening? I thought that you must be feeling bad, so I convinced Sundar to come with me to see you. There were quite a few students who listened when the guard came and told me, 'Ma'am says she is not in...'" Nick choked and could not speak for a while.

As Sumi started to apologize, Nick spoke again, "At least you could have come down or sent someone!"

Sumi's explanations and apologies did not make much difference. Nick went away, holding a grudge, and Sumi was left holding guilt.

"Well! One more feather in my life's lessons basket," she mumbled. She wrote that night in her diary before she slipped into her lonely world.

With that, she remembered reading about the greatest symbol, the lotus flower, of Eastern philosophy. The book had said, "The drops of water fall on the petals, but they simply slide off. Be like a lotus: remain untouched by the mud below and water above, and you are in control. Remain untouched, and you are the master."

She felt enveloped in a warm inner embrace that made her feel as though she was not alone.

> The thoughts are there, but less agitation.
> The feelings of pain, with time they will wane.
> The waves of life will rise and fall.
> I must remain, like a lotus in the rain."

Sumi did not want to share that bitter experience with anyone. So she did not dwell much on Minu's lies and her own embarrassment. She spoke some angry words to Minu and forgave her when she promised not to lie again. The cold relationship continued, but no one noticed the distance between them.

One good thing came out of that incident. Sumi realized how trustworthy and loyal Nick was, and their friendship flourished.

The Christmas holidays were uneventful at home. Priya had come to her parents' home with her sweet little boy, the joy of her life. Sumi had not taken care of any infant before. She was very unsure about how she felt about children, physically or emotionally.

One day, Sumi was spoon-feeding cereal and milk to Priya's little boy. She put one spoonful in his mouth, and he started to choke and cough. Sumi started screaming, thinking he would stop breathing and die! Priya came running, wiped his face, and laughed. It was nothing serious, but for Sumi, the fretful thought lingered. That feeling had taken a complicated turn in her head. She started to analyze her intentions...

Did she want to hurt the baby? Was she jealous, or was she wholeheartedly happy for Priya?

It was so strange. She could not talk to anyone. But indirectly, she talked to her mother, who smiled and said, "Do you know why you feel so confused? You know, first you had to share your friend with her husband, and now with her child. The insecurity in you clouds your perception. This happens. Don't worry about it. You will completely resolve this fear when you have your own child."

Sumi scolded herself for being so silly. She told herself, "In any relation, lack of trust starts from within, but it spreads the bitterness upon the sweet love…So be aware!"

One Step Forward

She returned for the last semester of school and focused on performing well on her final exams. Sumi felt free from the entanglements of any new relations or emotional dramas. She just cherished her time and enjoyed her friends. She knew that some of them she might never see again.

One Sunday afternoon, she was pleasantly surprised by her uncle when he showed up at her hostel without notice. He told Sumi to get dressed up to go and visit his friend. Sumi put on her best outfit to go out with her favorite mamu. On the way to his friend's house, Sumi remembered that first day alone in this city. She noticed the elegant neighborhood and gorgeous houses, which she had missed that day under the fog of her worries.

Mr. Sam Mody, her uncle's friend, said, "I apologize for putting you in trouble, but we were out of town. Your arrival information letter was not looked at. My servant told me later that you had no other place to go."

Her uncle said, laughing, "And anyway, your sons would have been too shy to ask her to stay here if they would have been home."

Sumi told him about her good experience with the stranger and that she had been okay in the hostel. They were engaged in a very interesting conversation when a young man entered the room. He was introduced as Mr. Sam's older son, Raju. When Sumi looked at him, their eyes were locked a little longer than normal.

Before Sumi was dropped off at her hostel, her uncle provided many details about Raju. Her uncle said Raju had finished the better part of his research work and was set to go to Stanford University in California to finish his thesis. Sumi entertained a wishful thought of seeing him again.

> Maybe once or twice in my whole lifetime
> I meet someone, like wind meets chime.
> The unknown vibrations like bells with the jangle.
> The tunes of my heart get twirled in a tangle.

Sumi ordered her mind to concentrate on her studies. As soon as her exams were over, she had planned to visit her cousin Risa in Mumbai.

Risa and her mother went to live with her grandfather's family after Risa lost her own father. Over the years, Sumi considered Risa the sister of her heart. Risa, a loyal cousin, filled the empty place of a missing sister for Sumi. They enjoyed their time together even though Sumi felt out of place in her grandfather's house.

The highlight of her trip was a visit to Priya at her in-laws' house where she was glad to receive a warm welcome by more than a dozen family members. Priya ruled like a queen, especially with her husband, when they were away from the other family members.

While she was in Mumbai, Sumi heard the good news that she was awarded a national scholarship toward her PhD. She returned home and joined the research institute in her city. Sumi was eager and energized to work on her special project.

The world around her was shining gently in the rising sun. She lived at home, went to work in the lab, and met new people. She could not explain why all those ordinary things seemed extraordinary. The tantalizing thought kept her on edge that…someone new would bump into her at the next corner. At twenty-two, she thought she was too old, while loved ones kept telling her, "You are too young to understand the realities of this complicated life."

One spring morning, Sumi's uncle stopped by and whispered to Sumi, "My friend's son Raju is coming to town tomorrow, and you are the reason for his visit. He is going to the USA next month."

They wanted to keep the prospects of meeting Raju a secret from Sumi's father. They were not sure that Raju's visit would lead to anything serious. Lucky for Sumi, her brother was in town for a week. So the next day, Sumi and her brother went to meet Raju at his lodge. They were feeling awkward and could not decide how to start the conversation.

Sumi started by asking him about his parents. Then she asked, "When I was at your home, I noticed a painting with your name on it. So you are an artist and a scientist, right?" That comment put Raju at ease, and an innate calm adorned his face. Unpretentiously, he started to ask some questions.

Raju seemed curious to know, so he remarked, "Your uncle told me you play a musical instrument!"

Sumi modestly replied, "Yes, I learned to play sitar for a couple of years. Even though I have passed three exams, I am far from performing on any stage. My personal preference is singing, and I went to our city's music center for vocal training in my teenage years." She confessed to herself that she had been neglecting further training lately.

With that reply, Raju's face lit up, and he started to talk about Indian classical music. His enthusiasm was contagious, and Sumi was easily pulled into the flow of the conversation. Raju realized that Sumi was genuinely interested in music.

Sumi's brother stepped out of the room to meet someone. Raju said with a smile, "I will share this with you since I see your interest in music. I went to Pundit Ravishankar's sitar concert. A couple was seated next to me. The husband was fully engrossed in the music, while the wife was asleep. At that point, I decided that I would choose a partner who could share my love of music and would not be so uninterested during these magical experiences."

Sumi and Raju talked effortlessly. When her brother returned, they went to Sumi's house where her mother was anxiously waiting to meet and greet Raju. Sumi could tell that her mom was intently studying Raju's body language. She was mentally prepared to hear her mom's keen evaluation.

Sumi suggested taking him to a library to show him the volumes of the most beautiful Kangra-style paintings. The next day, Raju came to pick up Sumi at her research lab. It was noontime, and Minu was covering for the front desk receptionist. Raju inquired about Sumi, and in a very friendly, inquisitive way, Minu introduced herself as Sumi's friend. When Sumi came down, Minu had already gathered plenty of information about the good-looking young scientist. As they walked out, Minu showed thumbs-up sign, but Sumi felt a jealous look behind it.

Sumi took Raju to a very special library and proceeded with familiarity in that place. She brought some volumes to the table, and they both admired the paintings. At the same time, they felt lively presence of each other sitting there side by side. Raju was observing Sumi's authentic interest as they were reading the details about the Kangra paintings.

In the inspiring environment of the Himachal Pradesh with the beautiful green hills, wavelike terraced paddy fields, and rivulets fed with the glacial waters of the snow-covered Dhauladhar, the Mughal style with sensitive naturalism blossomed into the Kangra style. Instead of painting flattering portraits of their masters and hunting scenes, the artists adopted themes from love poetry of Jayadeva, Bihari, and Keshavdas, who wrote ecstatically of the love of Radha and Krishna.

Kangra painting is an art both of line and color. A vigorous rhythmical line is the basis of this art. It is also an art of color, and the artists reveled in the use of pure blues, yellows, reds, and greens. These paintings are really fossils of a culture, which, when studied and interpreted, tell us more about the historical past than the records of travelers.

One striking feature of the ancient Indian Kangra paintings is the verdant greenery it depicts. The style is naturalistic, and great attention is paid to detail. The foliage depicted is vast and varied in Kangra paintings. This is made noticeable by using multiple shades of green. The Kangra paintings feature flowering plants and creepers, leafless trees, rivulets, and brooks. Another striking feature is that Kangra paintings depict the feminine charm in a very graceful manner. Facial features are soft and refined. The female figures are exceptionally beautiful.

The conversation took on a serious tone at the restaurant over the pistachio ice cream. They talked about their goals and dreams. Sumi made mental notes to see the possibilities of this match. The time flowed like an enchanting stream. Finally, the bustling of the customers reminded them to vacant the table.

Raju wanted to see his grandfather's house where he had stayed for a couple of years when he was in high school. They walked to the old neighborhood. They decided to sit on a bench facing a huge cricket field. Raju seemed very nostalgic, remembering the games his brother and he used to play with other kids.

"I was the cricket gang leader and owned the equipment. My younger brother, Jay, used to take advantage of that. He would come and insist upon batting and soon used to get clean-bowled by the older bowler. He would throw the bat and run way. He knew that I would not reprimand him…my mischievous brother," he said. Sumi was touched by the sound of that gentle sentence. She exactly knew the tender feelings for a brother.

Sumi turned her head toward Raju, and they gazed into each other's eyes. The sweet silence was murmuring in the shadow of the twilight. The temple bells were chiming far away, singing the song of evening. The clouds were colored with the orange rays of sunset at the distant horizon.

On the way home, they met Priya. She had come to be with her family to celebrate Holi. It was obvious that she had been sitting on the porch, waiting for Sumi and Raju to pass by her house. Priya greeted them, smiling as she was aware of Sumi's feelings toward Raju.

"So, Rajubhai, when are you going to share your thoughts with us? My friend is not a very patient person," Priya blurted out. Sumi's face turned red with embarrassment.

But Raju gave a friendly smile and nodded, saying, "Very soon."

It was the last evening for Raju in town, and it was very important to have him meet Sumi's father. Sumi was pretty nervous as they headed home. After meeting Raju, her mother and brother were happy. Her mom was not saying much, and the siblings knew the meaning of that silence, "I approve."

Raju was introduced to her father. "He is from Vadodara, and Sumi has known him since last year."

They avoided telling her father that her mamu was the middleman. The modern thinking of her uncle might backfire because Raju was of a lower caste than Sumi's family, and they knew that it would be difficult for her father to accept a son-in-law from a lower-caste family. He might listen to Sumi's uncle later.

Shortly after the introduction, Raju left with some change in his pace as he walked away. Sumi's heart ached to see him go. All were quiet in their own confusion…Her mother decided to talk more about the subject the next morning.

Sumi's heart was fluttering like the wings of a hummingbird. She could not comprehend her own sentiments.

Moist Petals

Misty sweet dreams, come sleep beside me.
The shades of the rainbow, I have yet to see.
My topsy-turvy mind! Enough of this ploy,
Rest and relish, there are moments to enjoy.

The Resistance

Her mother started to say, "Sumi likes Raju…"

Before she could finish her sentence, Sumi's father asked, "I can figure out by his last name, Mody, a Vaishya. He is not a Brahmin. Is that right?" The disappointment in his voice sounded deep and disturbing.

"Yes, but family is very cultured and highly educated." Januma tried her best to build Sumi's case.

"I say they are lower caste than us. You will marry a Brahmin. That's the way it is," Sumi's father reiterated.

"But what Krishna says in the Gita about the caste system is, 'The fourfold order in the society was created according to the divisions of quality and work.'" Sumi said.

Bhagavad Gita explains in chapter 4, Sanskrit shlok 13,

चातुर्वण्य मया सृष्टं गुणकर्मवभिागशः ।
तस्य कर्तारमपि मां वद्धियकर्तारमव्ययम् ॥४-१३॥

Sattva guna predominates in *Brahmins*. Their tasks (karma) are to study Vedas and perform sacred religious rituals, etc.

Rajas guna predominates in *Kshatriyas*. Sattva guna is secondary. Their karma is to be warriors and show bravery and tejas.

Rajas guna also predominates in *Vaishyas*. Tamas guna is secondary. Their karma is to be farmers and traders.

Tamas guna predominates in *Shudra*. Rajas guna is secondary. Their karma is to serve others.

The emphasis is on guna (aptitude) and karma (function) and not on jaati (birth). The varna, or the order to which we belong, is independent of sex, birth, or breeding. A varna is determined by temperament and vocation—not by birth or heredity. According to the Mahabharata, the whole world was originally of one class, but later, it became divided into four divisions on account of the specific duties.

Even after knowing the facts that Raju's father was an engineer, not a farmer or trader, Sumi's father vehemently objected to any further consideration of this proposal—because he belonged to a Vaishya caste...The wings were tied before the dream bird began to fly.

The magical moments and smiling eyes,
A clear milky way could lead to paradise...
But alas!
The stones of doubts were rolled in her way.
Now she tumbled and wondered to turn
which way?

Sumi was drowning in the flood of emotions, and an overwhelming voice echoed, "I should not hurt my father's feelings."

On the other hand, Sumi told herself to calm down. She thought, *Raju has not said yes yet. Why aggravate the situation! The storm of emotions may die down in a few days, and my life will go back to the good old boring routine.*

However, the next evening turned uglier at her house. When her father came home, he was angrier than the previous day. Sumi realized that he must have discussed the situation with his orthodox friends and come back with even stronger opposition. He made clearer that marriage with Raju would give Sumi a bad name and bring shame to the family.

Sumi tried to keep her mind on her work, but it would wander off, and she had to bring it back from all over the place. She was waiting for some response from Raju, but when his letter finally arrived, she was full of despair just looking at it.

"What are you worried about? Just open the letter," her brother said. But she knew that, either way, it would give her pain. Hesitantly, she opened his letter. She was mesmerized by the full page written in his beautiful handwriting...Sumi started to read, forgetting to breathe.

Raju had thanked everyone. He had discussed very candidly about the serious matters, like her father's possible objections and the uncertainty of his future plans. She was encouraged when she read the last line.

I am thinking positively and hope to meet you again, soon.

All these years, she used to sing those emotional, sad film songs. But that day, she felt them very close to her heart as she held back tears like a fragile wall of clay holds back the flooding river. A sympathetic look or a kind word was enough to make her cry.

She ran to Priya, and sobbing, she told her about her dilemma. She was being pulled mercilessly in two directions. "My first obligation is to respect my father's wishes and make him proud of me. But my soul is rebelling fiercely to break away from the confinement of their blind beliefs." Sumi rested her head on Priya's shoulder.

Slowly, she lifted her head with some decision. Priya also realized that Sumi had to nip this in the bud. She liked Raju, but she convinced herself that she could not trample on her father's heart to save this new relationship...It was not a longtime love affair or anything like that...Her mother and brother did not share her father's beliefs, but Sumi felt that they would not be able to change her papa's mind.

Sumi talked to her uncle and mother about her reply to Raju. She was confused about what to write. Her brother came up with the line, "I have no inclination...," and the letter was mailed. She was halfheartedly feeling relieved and, at the same time, gloomy.

The next letter came very quickly. It was short and sharp. Raju wrote,

> *You may look back and reexamine your response and words. Even your friend expressed how you felt about me. And now you are saying that...you have no inclination! I know this response is coming from a loving daughter who is obeying her father's wishes unwillingly. Even though you do not agree with his attitude, you fail to show enough courage to stand on your own free, independent thoughts.*

Oh! Those words hurt her like a prickly cane, but she had to face the facts. Her mother observed how Sumi was silent and seemed lost within. She waited patiently for Sumi to come to her to talk about the dilemma, but days passed by, and Sumi remained aloof.

The doorbell rang one afternoon. Sumi opened the door and was flabbergasted.

"Ajay! What are you doing here?" And impulsively, she hugged him.

"I have come here to see my future sister-in-law, *maybe*?" he said with a mischievous grin.

Raju had mentioned his brother Jay's nickname at home. So Sumi had no clue. But Ajay had realized that Sumi was the same girl whom he had met two years ago in Vadodara and had called her didi, the older sister.

He had informed Sumi's brother secretly that he was in town for his friend's wedding and would stop by to see them. Sumi was overwhelmed to find out that Ajay was Raju's brother.

> Her face was a blossom of joy,
> like a rose in the spring
> ...tickled by the gentle breeze.

They were enjoying his visit until Sumi's father came home. Before Sumi's mother exited to the kitchen, Ajay handed her a letter. "My mother sent this."

The young trio continued to talk in the front room.

After about fifteen minutes, Ajay went inside, said his good-byes, and proceeded to catch a bus. Sumi and her brother decided to accompany him to the bus stop. All of a sudden, they were startled to hear their father's voice.

"Sumi! Stop right now. I will take poison if you will disobey me." Sumi and her brother were mortified. They could not understand why her father was behaving like that at that time. He gave a stern look, turned back, and walked away.

Sumi said some muffled parting words to Ajay and walked back. Some people nearby watched the free show with interest. When they came home, her father was in his room behind a closed door. Their mother explained what had happened.

"I read their mother's letter, which describes Raju as a very good person. She also wrote that they would have no problem if Sumi and Raju quietly want to get married," Mother said.

Sumi's mom had put the letter down and gotten busy in the kitchen. Her father had walked in, picked up the letter, and read it. Somehow, he had assumed that Sumi was going away to meet Raju that night. That thought had enraged him, and he had come after them, shouting.

Over the next few days, Sumi became submerged in a deep ocean of misery, barely breathing. The sadness was overwhelming, and people noticed. One day, Minu shamelessly inquired about Raju. Frustrated, Sumi harshly responded.

"Why are you asking me these questions? You will be happy to know that nothing is happening between Raju and me. Are you satisfied?" Sumi said. Minu turned red and angrily walked away without a word. Sumi murmured, "Good riddance!" Minu was curt with Sumi for some time. Then all of a sudden, Sumi noticed a peculiar smile on her face. Sumi tried to guess, but nothing really seemed obvious, so she decided to ignore her smug look. Sumi's life was back to her normal, boring routine.

She did not hear from Raju after the incident. She assumed, "Raju must have given up after hearing from his brother about my father's threats."

My eyes wish to see who was here for a
while.
We met like a dream and separated like a
shadow.
My soul is tugged so tender and agile.
He trails beside, but how to touch, can't
decide.

Silent Sorrow

No two snowflakes are alike. It is as true as no two men are alike. The tiniest shift in temperature or moisture changes a flake's unique shape…

> The flakes fall heavier, whirling in the wind. Human noises evaporate; now nobody moves. Snow comes to earth and forms snow lampposts, snow trees, snow cars, snowmen. New worlds appear and disappear, leaving their prints upon our imagination. But when the snow melts away, the lampposts are unmoved, untouched; just like our traditions.

Sumi found her soul in the center of a storm, stirred by her mind. She thought, *How in the world does my father feel the caste system is so important that he cannot see the person beyond? It is a dark veil of prejudice! I see it as clearly as a bright sunny day: all human beings are the same. The separation is the result of crooked minds.*

The months passed, with Sumi in a somber mood. Sumi was encouraged by her father to accept candidates from their caste.

"My friend's son is well educated and has a good job. If you marry him, I would build a house for you, right here on this land."

It is ironic, Sumi thought. *I dream to fly around the world, and Papa is trying to tempt me with a cage!*"

Sumi met some new prospects, but she could not help but compare them to Raju, and her heart would cringe with the thought of being with someone else.

One Sunday afternoon, the much-discussed topic again resurfaced in her family conversation. Sumi was reminded that the midtwenties was the upper age limit for a girl to be unmarried. Her eyes were in a book, but she was not reading. Her face looked serene, but the flames were lurking behind. She was feeling depressed. At that time, her neighbor's child came and announced, "Sumi, my mom wants you to come to our house."

"When and why?" Sumi asked.

"Right now, and I don't know," he said and ran.

Sumi reluctantly complied and showed up at the neighbor's house. But she was pleased to see her neighbor's distant relative, none other than her friend Nick!

"Hello! Are you surprised? That was my plan," Nick said, smiling.

"Yes, I am. It has been a couple of years since we last saw one another. How are you?" she said.

Sumi was glad to see him, but her pleasure was like a half-moon, partially covered with some gray shadows.

They talked about everything and everyone they knew, even Sundar. Nick informed her that Sundar was happily married and was settled in Mumbai. Sumi silently wished him well and then said, "The lessons in life are hard to handle at times, but those events make us stronger and help us to clear our vision."

The hostess seemed bored with the unfamiliar chatter. When she went inside, Nick leaned in and whispered, "Sumi! Do you have time to talk with me?"

She nodded. "Yes."

As soon as his aunt returned, Nick said, "Excuse me, Aunty, I have to take your leave."

"Oh, okay. Glad you came by!" And she waved good-bye to both of them, with a curious look on her face.

"So you know that I have come to see you!" Nick said to Sumi. If it would not have been for Sumi, Nick would not have had any reason to visit those relatives.

After many years, now Sumi and Nick had a very special kind of friendship. Nick would go out of his way to do things for her, while Sumi had taken him for granted many times. She appreciated his attention, and she felt a certain calm and trust between them.

"So what's on your mind?" Sumi asked with a gentle smile.

"You know that my cousin Renu got married a few months ago," Nick said.

"Oh! Yes. I felt bad that I could not attend her wedding. I want to see her soon."

Nick smiled. "Okay. That has been arranged. Renu has invited you for dinner tomorrow evening. She and her husband have moved into a new house, which is not too far from here."

"I would love to come," Sumi replied. Then there was silence except for the slow beat of their footsteps.

Sumi waited patiently. All of a sudden, Nick spoke as if a puff of energy had pushed him.

"This is like…a now-or-never question. I got a job in Bangalore."

"Very nice! I am impressed. Congratulations," Sumi exclaimed.

"My parents want me to get married soon." Nick stopped and turned to look at Sumi. "You know that I like you or, as they tease me, am devoted to you. I heard from Ajay that you had an open and shut encounter with his brother. My question to you is, do you see any possibility of our future together?" Nick hesitantly asked.

Sumi was somewhat surprised and slightly nervous. *What timing!* Sumi thought. Just that morning, she had been given a reminder of the "age limit" for getting married. She was depressed and desperate, and then this proposal came.

"I don't know what to say," she pensively said. "I am deeply touched by your proposal, and I will think about it. But right now, I cannot say anything." She managed to deliver the sentences in one breath.

Nick replied with a faint smile. "Sure, take your time. But I know that in this sort of matter, if you have to think about it, I can already guess the answer."

"You know that this was a bit sudden for me." Sumi was sensing his pain and anxiety.

"Don't worry. I will not fall apart. I am your friend, and that fact will not change," Nick said calmly. Sumi could see that he had come prepared.

They talked some more while they walked back to her house. They warmly held each other's hands. Two beautiful eyes looked at the sober face kindly. She tried to give an encouraging look but did not know if she succeeded.

Sumi entered the gate of her house. She turned to close the gate and saw Nick looking in her direction longingly. Sumi waved at him.

Sumi went straight to her room. This proposal brought a different kind of confusion for her. This person, whom she had known for several years, had shown sincere care for her. He had a job! He was a Brahmin too. The situation would be convenient for her. It would please her parents and would resolve the problem.

Sumi chuckled. "And they will stop singing, 'How do you solve a problem like Sumia?'"

Sumi thought, *This is too good. Now if only I can convince my heart and my oddball head. But they are too stubborn and do not understand how good this opportunity is…I'll have to talk to my brother.*

But he has not met Nick yet! Well, even so…

She put off all thoughts and decisions until the next day and came out of her room, almost running.

Her mother noticed the change and was happy to see the brightened face after a long time.

The next day, before she went, Sumi told her mother, "I am going to meet Nick at Renu's house. Yesterday evening, he asked me a question about the possibility of our future together. I am thinking about it, but I haven't decided my reply. As you say, at the right moment, my heart and mind will play the same tune, and I'll have an answer."

Mom looked at her confident and wise daughter. She told Sumi, "Just in case they are out of tune, come to Mama. By the way, this pink sari looks good on you."

Sumi smiled in agreement and reminded her brother to come to pick her up on time. Sumi had thought that she would reply to Nick after her brother met him later that evening. Shan had completed his education and had joined an engineering company in their city. It was a super comfort for Sumi to have her brother at home. Her family had also started looking for a good match for her brother.

Sumi met Renu's husband for the first time.

He seemed like a nice guy. He enthusiastically showed their new house. When Sumi went in the kitchen to help out, Renu said, "I have observed that my cousin Nick adores you. I hope he does not start to believe of getting more from you than he is ever going to get." She heard a protective tone in her voice.

"What! Why do you say that?" Sumi was taken aback.

"I know you well, and I know that you are a free-flying soul. You will not compromise if you are not fully convinced. Please take this comment as a compliment," Renu said softly.

Why do people think they know me better than I know myself? Whom should I trust more? Sumi thought.

After the pleasant evening and delicious dinner, Sumi and Nick stepped out on the front porch to wait for her brother. Somehow, Renu's comment had compelled Sumi to think clearly. She did not want to mislead Nick.

"So I will be leaving tomorrow morning. Do you have any definite answer for me? Or if you need more time, it is okay with me," Nick said, trying to keep the conversation as light and simple as possible.

Sumi spoke without any premeditated plan, "You have been a very good friend, and I really value that, but I cannot imagine any other relationship between us." She observed Nick's expression and continued, "What I am saying right now is coming spontaneously from my heart. So it must be a proper decision for both of us. Do you agree?"

"This was not the expected answer, but the way you put it seems to be the correct decision. Our camaraderie has evolved in a spiral fashion." With an amusing smile, Nick continued, "You really disliked me in the beginning—no need to deny it. We are at a crossroads, and whichever path we choose would be balanced on a loyal friendship. We will always have a special bond."

Sumi replied, "I am so glad for your visit. I am thankful for your candid approach to these feelings. If left unsaid, it could have really hurt our friendship."

The deep gray twilight was lowering its blanket while stars were trying to peek in randomly with their bright eyes.

"I feel so relieved and optimistic for my future now. Whomever I will choose, I will be totally committed to that person," Nick said.

"I don't know about me, but I am sure you will settle with the right life partner and will be a good family man."

In the distance, Sumi saw her brother coming. She smiled and said, "I was to discuss your proposal with my brother, but as Renu said, my free-flying soul did not need any help in making this decision."

They promised to keep in touch and cheerfully said farewell to each other.

She closed a chapter, but his friendship left
a mark.
The book was still open, with a silky
bookmark.

Sumi introduced her brother to Nick. After some polite conversation, they were on their way home.

Sumi was chattering away as if nothing out of the ordinary had happened. Her brother had sensed her answer to Nick as they were saying good-bye.

Exasperated, her brother remarked, "Sumi! You make big decisions too quickly. Why did you have to decline this nice offer? Do you know why some people are successful and some are not? When opportunity comes, some grab it with both hands, and some don't lift a finger. I hope you don't regret this later. He seemed like a good fellow."

Sumi quietly contemplated her brother's concerns. She reexamined her thoughts and said, "Bhai, you are right that I made the decision quickly. But I tried to listen to my inner voice, and I did not hear, 'Yes,' coming from anywhere."

"You and your inner voice will drive everybody crazy." He laughed, and Sumi joined him.

Awakening

"Isn't it great that I have the choice to say yes or no? I can't stop thinking about the old rigid rules of the society where women had no choice and had to take orders and obey the men at the every stage of her life. As a woman, I understand the silent sorrow of the suppressed souls," Sumi said.

Shan listened silently. Sumi continued, "I will have to share this with you from Kahlil Gibran's book *The Broken Wings*. His love, Selma, was compelled to marry the bishop's nephew. Gibran wrote, 'Thus destiny seized my Selma and led her like a humiliated slave, and thus fell that noble spirit into the trap after having flown freely on the white wings of love in a sky full of moonlight scented with the fragrance of flowers.'"

Her brother appreciated the deep understanding behind her decision to decline Nick's marriage proposal.

"And, brother! One more thing before we go in the house. I did not make a quick decision about Raju, remember?" Her voice was tinged with sadness.

"Because you heard the clamor of conflicting inner voices, is that not true?" He tried to make lighter tone of it. All of a sudden, Sumi's eyes were moist, and Shan noticed that. He thought, *She has not forgotten Raju.*

That weekend, Sumi's family was busy with her cousin's wedding. Many relatives from her father's side were in town. From the early morning, everybody had to sit there and suffer through the sacramental ceremonies. She had no faith or interest in those senseless rituals.

Among all those elder relatives, Sumi's mother was the only college graduate. With her personality and grace, it did not seem like Januma belonged there. But she was very cordial with the kin, and everyone respected her. The hours expended with all those relatives seemed futile to Sumi. After simple inquiries, they had nothing more to talk about. She observed that her father was trying to impress these people. He wanted to show that his children, even though highly educated, followed tradition.

It was late afternoon. The noise of loud music and the chanting of the shlokas by priests were intermingled with the nonstop chattering around her. Sumi had an awakening moment. Her mind was provoked.

What am I doing here? I am Sumi. There was no Sumi before, nor will be after. I am forcing to mold my entire being according to my father's thinking? He who does not care to see what I think or feel? These so-called relatives would not spare a sympathetic look if I were in trouble. Wake up, Sumi!

When they left, Sumi had a determined look on her rosy face. Her steps were momentous. Resonance filled her being: use your energy to serve your soul.

When mind and soul do not get along,
the trauma, turmoil will stay too long.
The moment one sees the futility of it all,
it begins to dissolve.
Vision brings the power of choice,
and conflicts resolve.

The time had come to tie up the loose ends of her research work. In reference to her thesis, Sumi had to go to Vadodara for one day and stay in Mumbai for a week. Her brother had come to the train station to see her off. At the last minute, Shan told Sumi, "Ajay knows by which train you are arriving in Vadodara. Don't refuse if he shows up at the station and wants to take you to their house. To my knowledge, Raju has not returned from the USA."

"Oh! Brother. Why to put them in a quandary?"

Her brother had no answer. But he felt that he had to do something. He could not ignore his sister's tender feelings smothered away under the rigid rules of the society. His look conveyed, "Let's see... what happens."

As the train was approaching the Vadodara station, Sumi was scanning for familiar faces and was praying that she would not see any at the same time. She had planned to stay in the hostel with a friend.

Sumi noticed one dignified couple. The man was in a white Nehru jacket, with a lovely lady wrapped in a beautiful sari. "Oh! Not Ajay…but his parents?"

Mr. and Mrs. Sam Mody were on the platform. Sumi wistfully thought, *They maybe traveling somewhere…Hope they don't see me.* Sumi gathered her luggage and proceeded to disembark.

They waved at her as soon as they spotted her.

"Namaste, Uncle and Auntie, I am surprised to see you here. Are you going somewhere?" Sumi greeted them respectfully.

"No. We have come to receive my friend's niece," Mr. Mody said with a jovial smile.

"I have made arrangements," Sumi said nervously.

"We know, but if you don't mind, please come with us. Consider our house as your own," Raju's mom convincingly said.

Sumi thought it would be rude to argue anymore. On the way, they asked about her family and her thesis. Sumi never felt any grudge on their side.

She walked into their home. It was a poetic morning, or that's how Sumi perceived it. In the rising sun, the dewdrops had just dried. The bright rays reflected on the green glossy leaves. The front porch was covered with the delicate white petals of parijat flowers. The loud music reached Sumi first, followed by Ajay's smiling sleepy face.

"Welcome, didi," he said with a soft hug. "I am glad to have you here, but note this: one day is a very short time."

"You are right, maybe next time. Today I have to meet my professor at ten o'clock, and then for the next five days, I will be in Mumbai," Sumi said.

She was escorted to her room. Sumi came out of her room, wearing a blue sari. The three family members greeted her with obvious admiration. They all enjoyed the scrumptious breakfast. Sumi had almost forgotten that she was meeting them for only the second time and maybe the last.

Ajay was to drop Sumi off at the university campus. His mom made sure that Sumi would return before dinnertime.

Sumi could not bring up Raju's name. She was all ears when Ajay said, "Rajubhai is returning from abroad any day. He would not give us the exact date of his arrival so Mom would not be apprehensive."

"Good," Sumi said, putting away the information in a special corner of her mind.

Sumi returned to their house in the early evening. At the dinner table, Mr. Mody talked about his college adventures with Sumi's uncle. They sat and talked about everything at the table for hours. It was very kind of them not to ask any questions about her father and his outburst.

Before Sumi went to bed, she stood by the window, enjoying the view of the garden surrounding a charming swing. The fragrance of the night jasmine glided around her. She had had a long day and fell asleep as soon as she put her head on the pillow.

It was a misty morning. Sumi got up and wrapped a woolen shawl around her shoulders. She saw herself sitting on the swing, lost in thought. She sensed a gentle movement next to her and an arm on her shoulder. She looked into Raju's eyes and smiled. He beamed.

...And she woke up, astonished.

Sumi had to catch the morning train. As she bid everyone good-bye, she bent and touched the elders' feet for blessings. She kept on looking at the gracious couple until she turned the corner. The affectionate exchange, though short, was deep and sweet.

There is no explanation given why you connect with some people, where time and circumstances do not matter.

> The flowers and thread tie side by side.
> The waves and wind twine tide by tide.
> Love flows naturally, no need to guide.
> The warm affection that gracefully glides

She left that house with mixed feelings. Their kindness raised her spirit, but sorrow followed. *I may not see them again*, she thought.

The train journey from Vadodara to Mumbai seemed shorter than usual. During the journey, she had time to think. It was a period of insecurity and uncertainty. Sumi was asking, "What should I do?"

The questions and opposition, the struggle and trials were not pinning her down, but they were the wind beneath her wings to soar up high. She was feeling so light; she could not wait to put one foot in front of the other in the race of life.

The wise men say, "As the ego is no longer running your life, you are able to live with uncertainty, even enjoy it. The acceptance may open up infinite possibilities. It means fear is no longer a dominant factor in your action."

Luck by Chance

In Mumbai, Priya and her husband had offered to pick Sumi up and drop her off at the lodge, near the university campus. As soon they sat in the car, Priya said, "Here is chai tea and snacks for you."

"I am starved. But my hunger sense had total faith that my dear friend Priya would come loaded with my favorite food. No one can feed me better." Sumi threw her arms around Priya. Her little boy was looking at them bashfully. Sumi turned to him. "Sweetheart! How is your baby sister, Tanya? I can't wait to see her."

Holding her son close, Priya said, "I can't wait to show her off. She is so…cute."

"Sumi! She has become one crazy mama," her husband said. Priya sweetly sulked as they laughed.

Sumi's work was finished by the end of the week, and she went to Priya's house for the weekend. She put away her suitcase and admired the sleeping baby. Priya pulled her to sit on the bed and eagerly asked, "How was your stay in Vadodara? They loved you, right?"

Sumi was all smiles. "I suppose so. I liked them too." She told her all the details and also about her early morning dream when she saw Raju seated next to her on a swing.

"Raju's mom invited me to come again."

"Oh, that's even better. Isn't this wonderful?"

"What is so wonderful? Nothing has changed on my side. My father's dislike of this union, the main obstacle, remains the same."

"I have a gut feeling that things will work out," Priya said. Sumi felt happy and grateful for her friend's positive input. The joyful chattering continued until they were called to go to the main room.

"Wait, before we go out, I have to tell you something." Priya stopped Sumi. "I ran into your friend Anu last week. She is appointed in Mumbai as the income tax officer. She will take charge officially on the first of next month. She has gone back to Delhi, to her mother's house this week. She told me that she has legally separated from her husband," Priya almost whispered.

"I know, so sad! She had not gone back to Kullu for several months. It was inevitable." Sumi knew about Anu's marital problems. It was a matter of time when she would walk away. Sumi had had to shift her mind from the troubling news before she went out to meet Priya's family.

About half a dozen family members gathered in the main room, and the afternoon session lasted until dusk. Priya's younger sisters-in-law were intrigued with Sumi's stories.

"One time, a doctor had come all the way from overseas to find a bride from our clan. He had heard some good things about me, so he showed up at our house. My parents were impressed. So what if he was not too tall? They sent him to my lab anyway. The young man saw a short pretty girl and another tall shabbily dressed workaholic while peeping inside the lab. He asked, 'Which one is Miss Sumi?' He was crushed when someone pointed at me." They laughed more when Sumi said, "The doctor still wanted to pursue the possibility, but I knew the 'odd-couple' pairing would not work for me."

All those jokes were for their merriment. But Sumi knew that in a real relationship, the shape of one's nose, height, or the color of skin would not play a critical role in life. She should never mislay her focus from what she was looking for in her partner.

The next day, Sumi had to catch the late evening train. Priya had a big spread on the dining table and lovingly insisted Sumi eat more. Afterward, good-byes took much longer. By the time they arrived at the station, only a few minutes were left for Sumi to find her compartment. She hugged Priya at the gate and hurried to find her seat. Through the train's whistle and in the bustle of people all around her, she heard a voice calling her name. She stopped but was hesitant to look back. She thought this could be a delusion.

"Sumi! Sumi, wait." She heard a man's voice.

Is that Raju?

Yes, he was standing at the door, one compartment behind. Sumi walked back quickly and said, "Hi!… Uh, I have to find my reserved seat."

Raju stepped down and suggested timidly, "If you don't mind, my cabin is almost empty. I would like to talk to you, if possible…"

Sumi had to decide quickly. In agreement, she extended her arm to hand him her suitcase. Raju stepped back and then followed her carrying the suitcase. There was only one other couple in the cabin.

Near the gate, Priya was looking with wide eyes and was waving excitedly. Sumi prayed that Raju would not see the display of her over exuberance.

The blissful friendship is embossed with
trust.
The loyalty and love adorn it first.
In the dark, she finds the star that twinkles.
In heat, she mists the cool, kind sprinkles.
This life of mine feels rich inside.
The rest may oppose, but a friend stays
beside.

With a shrill whistle, the train began to roll. Sitting across from Raju, Sumi felt so awkward that she started to scold herself for agreeing to his impromptu invitation. She was wondering, *Now where to look?* Good thing she was sitting by the window. So she kept on looking at the passing buildings. Raju might have noticed her awkwardness, and a smirk appeared at the corner of his lips. "Don't worry. I don't bite," he said.

Sumi laughed and said, "And that's why I agreed to travel in your compartment," half convincing herself.

Sumi thought, *How uncomplicated he seems. There is no harm in talking with him. I am not committing any crime or hiding anything from my parents. Now I have to take a deep breath so my crazy beating heart can slow down.* She tried to concentrate on the rhythm of the moving train.

"So how is your thesis work going?" Raju asked.

"Oh, it seems like a never-ending task. It is like writing a novel. You go back again and again to add or edit. The big difference is, for the thesis, you are accountable for each word of every line," Sumi said.

"I know. The weight feels overwhelming at times…But it will be over, and you will look back and wonder, 'How did I manage to do all this?'"

"Noted. So the qualified Doctor Raju states." Sumi chuckled.

Sumi sat back and relaxed. They were meeting after more than two years, but she had seen this face in the mirror of her mind countless of times. She realized that she had put on an old shirt over jeans. She mulled over, *I should have worn something decent. And my hair is all out of place. I did not even check in the mirror before leaving Priya's house. I may look horrible. Oh, I hope he stops staring at me.*

Her rampant imagination had masked her senses. To distract him from her appearance, she inquired about his stay in the USA.

"It was great except I missed my family and Mom's cooking. I was fortunate to attend some classical music concerts by top artists from India. Other than those exceptional evenings—my weekends, especially Sunday evenings, were spent alone with Talat Mahmood's songs."

"I know the feeling. When I was in the Vadodara dorm, Sunday evenings were quite lonely, no boyfriend and no family."

They both were talking about things, but were thinking about something else. Sumi was agonizing. *How to bring up the subject? Our time together will be over soon, and the unsaid words will hum and sting me like bees.*

Then Raju's question shook her up.

"Ajay told me about Nick's intention to ask you the big question. I suppose…things would have worked out between you two?"

"Nick and I are just friends. That issue has been cleared out smoothly." She staggered but continued. "I have been meeting some prospects since I did not hear from you after my father's eruption." After the quick response, Sumi uneasily smiled and waited for him to speak.

He looked confused as he said, "I don't get it. You never responded to my phone call."

"What phone call?" Sumi was puzzled.

"Okay, let me begin from the day Ajay returned after visiting your home and told me about what had happened. My first reaction was to close that door for good." Sumi listened with a painful knot in her gut. "But Ajay described the pleasant time he had with you, your brother, and mother. I considered some options, but my mind would not let me rest. I waited for two days expecting to feel at ease about the whole scenario."

"And you did get the peace, and you left for the USA." She heard a little whine in her own voice.

"Yes, I left, but not with any peace. I struggled in vain for two days. My parents tried to convince me to consider other girls. But after a long discussion, they concluded that I was too far gone over you. They were ready to help me in any way they could to resolve the conflicts. I had your work phone number, so I called. I was told that you were out of town and my message would be conveyed to you."

"I did not get any message." Sumi tried to remember. It was the beginning of her work schedule, and she did not go out of town, not even for one day. "There was some casual talk in our ladies' group about a wedding on my father's side of the family, which I could not attend."

"I heard the receptionist asking someone. Then she said, 'Her friend says Sumi is out of town, and she will convey the message that you called.' And that was it."

"I think Minu has struck again!" Sumi mumbled. Her voice drowned in the noise of the moving train.

After seeing the question in Raju's eyes, Sumi explained. "Do you remember meeting my so-called friend Minu at my lab?"

"Yes, vaguely." Raju nodded.

"Minu and I have a sour history, and to make the relationship worse, I had snapped at her when she repeatedly asked me about you and what was happening between us. So, out of spite, she must have made up that excuse. She never uttered a word about your phone call," Sumi concluded.

"I did not dare to talk to your uncle or anyone else before I could talk to you. Soon my departure date approached, and I had to leave. I thought you also may have some faith in the caste system." Raju took a deep breath.

"Wow! I assumed something different. I thought I might not be special enough for you to pursue the matter, or you got scared by one howl from the father lion!" Sumi said.

"I proved you wrong today by running after you and successfully bringing you here. You agree?"

In reply, Sumi shyly concurred.

> Some tried to place the heart of the day
> in the bosom of night.
> But the hand of destiny leads;
> where hearts understand each other
> and spirits mellow with revelation.

The White Lilies

The sun was spreading the last of its yellow shine before dipping into the horizon. Like the trail of trees, time was disappearing as the train was racing through the shadow of dusk. The Vadodara station was coming closer by the minute.

Sumi was wondering what to tell Raju in those few crucial minutes. Should she share her innermost feelings or put them away in the secret corner of her heart forever? Sumi wished that the train would just slow down. And it did slow down—because the station was approaching. They both were silent, each waiting for the other to speak.

Will the white lilies wilt,
before touched by his tender hand?
Will the snow flurries melt,
before the snowflakes convey how I felt?

Raju was intently looking at her ever-changing expressions. He was also in a deep dilemma. The other couple started to collect their luggage and proceeded to disembark. Lost in her thoughts, and obviously disappointed, Sumi said, "Your station has come."

She expected Raju to get ready to get down. "The train will start moving soon."

"That's okay." Raju got more comfortable in his seat. "I did not have the advance booking. So, at the last minute, I had to purchase what was available—a ticket up to the last terminal stop. Nobody is expecting me at home tonight. If you don't mind, I can continue my journey with you." He grinned at her, and Sumi shivered with a wave of a thrill in her body. She did not try to hide her pleasure.

The train started moving. The beat of her heart and the rhythm of the engine became a consonance of inner and outer music. Sumi looked at Raju, maybe for the first time, with an unwavering glance. She looked carefully at his full head of curly hair, the perfectly lined teeth, and two amorous eyes. When the other passenger asked some question, Raju replied with a kind smile. Raju turned his head to look back at Sumi and broke her trance.

"So what did you do after you did not get any assurance from me?" Raju inquired.

"Well! I was very sad for a few days. I assumed that nobody would like me enough to marry me anymore. I would die as an old maid."

"Oh! No!" Raju burst out laughing.

"And the day my uncle informed me that 'Raju went abroad,' a gloom wrapped around me. For several days, time floated aimlessly. Eventually, one day I went to see my music teacher to declare that I would devote my simple life to music and my education. I asked him to order a sitar for me."

Raju was overcome with emotion. He got up and sat next to Sumi. He held her hand tenderly. Sumi bashfully said, "My attempt to abstain from worldly pleasures did not last for too long. Fortunately, a rich student came along and purchased that expensive instrument." And she smiled.

"May I confess this? I could not put you out of my mind—your bright eyes and smiling face. During the classical music concerts, my mind used to drift away with the sound of some sensual ragas…thinking about you."

"What else did you remember?" she asked longingly.

"When I had asked you about your hobbies, you had replied, 'I like to sing.' Wow! What an answer. One more thing, I was touched by your affectionate relationship with your brother and other family members," he continued nostalgically.

"Even after that unsaid break up, my heart would not accept that you were gone for good. You were right there in the middle of my existence. My mute feelings were expressed in words by my brother. He had said, 'Sumi! You go to America for further studies and marry Raju over there to avoid the social pressure.' My mother was listening but did not express any protest against that idea. This little encouragement told me that they both liked you a lot." Sumi serenely sensed the warmth of his hand.

"I got so busy with my research work that I had hardly any communication with Ajay or anyone else."

Sumi smoothly pulled her hand back and said, "It has been more than two years. Didn't you get captivated by any gori girl, by the fair skin and blue eyes?"

"No. No one liked me enough to marry me either." Mockingly, he said, "Maybe they sensed that I was trapped in an invisible web."

The cool breeze of night was blowing with the speed of the train. Sumi's long hair was braided, but some strands were playing around her face. She was trying to control them. Raju helped her by putting a lock of hair behind her ear. He murmured, "The last time I saw you, I remember a pink rose like this in your hair. Today, I can enjoy the fragrance too." The petals of her lips curled up in a smile, and her grateful look thanked him for being there.

They shared the snack Priya had forcefully put in her suitcase. Raju said, "I will have to remember to thank your friend for this delicious feast. I have had a hard time finding good vegetarian food over there. I'm glad I am back."

"Me too."

She spoke in soft whispers, "In these few hours, I have become a different person. After this unexpected meeting, I feel my world has changed... to an unfamiliar comingling of affection and trust."

Sumi paused and looked into his passionate eyes. Raju silently waited as if he was engrossed in the music of her voice and wanted to hear more.

Sumi continued, "The words your mom said ten days ago I feel so true today. When I was leaving your home, she put her hand on my shoulder and said, 'Consider us as your family, and come again.' Oh! I want, wish, and pray to be a part of your family."

He sat up straight and said, "I wonder how these moments with you happened? We did not have any thread of connection between us for months and months. We run into each other and reconnect just like…two separated lovebirds!"

> Sprinkles of spring bring blossoms in the field.
> The soul meets the mate; with a stroke of fate.
> A droplet meets light, spreads a rainbow in the sky.
> Accept it, o my love, as a blessing in disguise.

From now on, each step would be taken with the recognition of their true feelings. They could see the path to their future more clearly. Sumi's heart was filled with excitement. Her whole being was stirred with joy. She had found a special love of her own.

Their emotions were running way ahead in the relay race of realities. They had realized how they felt about each other. All these words had come from the depth of their hearts.

Still the words resounded above the hum of the locomotive. "Raju, I confess to the fact that after meeting you, I could not convince myself to choose anyone else. But, at the same time, it would be heart-wrenching for me to walk away without my father's blessings. He is protesting against this relationship due to more concern for my reputation than his beliefs, even though the reason seems trivial in our minds."

Raju closed his eyes and leaned back. Sumi saw on his face the shades of anguish. Thoughtfully, he said, "We both know that we have something higher than just kinship and deeper than friendship. Where do we go from here?" Sumi had no straight answer for the question.

Raju spoke again, "I understand your agony. If I had to stand against my father's wishes, I don't know how I would handle it." He held her hand. "Tell me—what can I do to change your papa's mind?"

"I am sure if he opens his mind's window a little to know you, he would like you a lot. We have just found each other. Let's savor these moments."

Raju took Sumi's hand, placed his lips on it, and gave a long kiss. Her heart melted with that burning kiss, and she trembled with the sweet romantic tingles in her body.

"So let's see what we can accomplish together." Her determined look did not need more words.

The rest of the journey passed with conversation only between their eyes. Their hearts were beating through their fingers, and their souls were bonding with their pledge and promise, which only two lovers can confer.

The other passengers were sleeping, but those two awakened souls did not notice when the moonlit night merged with the early morning light. Sumi had never heard before the sweeter rhythm of a moving train or the hide-and-seek game of the moonlight with a man's face. They bonded with an invisible, unbreakable thread that was taking them to an insurmountable sphere.

Like any other journey, this romantic ride had to end. Raju helped Sumi in shifting to the connecting train, taking her to her hometown. They promised to write letters and, whenever possible, to call each other. They bade good-byes with heavy hearts.

Raju had to go out, to the ticket window, to purchase a return ticket to Vadodara. Sumi felt alone without him. The train's whistle announced its departure. The train started to move with a jerk. Sumi was looking out through the window and saw him coming toward her…Raju dropped his bag behind and came with a quick pace to hand her something.

"Oh how beautiful! The fresh, fragrant flowers of chrysanthemums! Thank you," Sumi exclaimed. She gave him a flying kiss, which he captured in his hand, closing his fingers around it. They kept on looking at each other. Just before her pretty face disappeared from his view, Raju saw two tears from her alluring eyes, falling on the flowers…as an obeisance.

Sumi's brother came to pick her up at the station. Sumi hugged Shan excitedly before he could take the suitcase from her hand. Shan was puzzled. "Wow! Sis! What's the matter? Did you miss me, or…did you win the lottery?"

She flashed a smile. "Yes, something like that."

"I guess it must be something to do with Raju."

"Well, do you think I don't have any other reason to smile?" Sumi asked.

"Nope! The way you are holding those flowers and this unruly smile—reveal your secret."

"Okay, you are correct. I will have to tell you all about my wonderful rendezvous." Sumi narrated her fairy-tale tryst, which her mind and heart had told each other several times in the last couple of hours.

When they entered their house, Sumi noticed her relatives were engrossed in some serious discussion with her parents. Their mother hurried her inside and said, "Shan didn't tell you? Remember that girl we had gone to meet with my friend? Shan and Sona want to get married. The discussion is about her family."

Her father's brother was warning against the girl's family. Her uncle said, "Her father is a well-known follower of Mahatma Gandhi. They live a very hard and simple life. Sometimes, he fights aggressively for his tenets. They could be very tough to deal with."

Januma rejoined the discussion. "I consider those as plus points. They live by noble principles. They do not believe in hoarding money." Her mother sounded animated with enthusiasm…

"We sincerely admire the way the whole family is devoted to her father's community service organization," Sumi pitched in.

"Uncle, they are not rough or a wild bunch of people. My papa has taught us the same lessons of truth and discipline. Both families follow similar Brahmin religious rituals. They are also vegetarian and strictly avoid alcohol. Sona and I are at the same wavelength," her brother said calmly.

"I agree with Shan. This will be a good union," their father said. Shan's speech and his papa's consent concluded the subject. Sumi and her brother exchanged a triumphant look as their father said good-bye to his brother.

The Seven Steps

Both families were happy when Sona and Shan chose to tie the knot. This was the best way for an arranged marriage to work out, like two flowers blossoming in the shade of surrounding trees.

"From now on, you are my chief negotiator. Are you up to this challenge?" Sumi said.

Shan saluted, "I accept the job."

"Naturally, you feel quite confident today. You are lucky that Sona is from a Brahmin family." Sumi was envious but very happy for her brother.

The priest looked at the couple's horoscopes, and based upon the position of the stars, the marriage date was finalized. Sumi showed her distrust in matching horoscopes and other fallacies, which constantly overshadow their daily lives in society.

"Do you want to follow this mumbo jumbo of horoscopes? Though the wedding date does suit my schedule, are you willing to wait a whole five months?" she commented to her brother.

"I don't give much importance to astrology, but I just go along with the rituals if I am not inconvenienced too much. If the right position of the stars makes

Ma and Papa happy, then why not?" he said. Sumi admired her easygoing, reverential brother.

"That means I have to start preparing my mind to sit patiently through your long…long wedding ceremony!"

"Yes, you better!" he replied, pretending to be a strict older brother.

Sumi's home was buzzing with excitement. The next day, the mother and daughter found some quiet time together. Sumi suggested they go up on the terrace to watch the sunset. The cool air was soothing on the warm day. They could hear the children playing and the sweet hymns from the neighbors' homes. The soft jingle of the bells was making the twilight enchanting.

"Ma, a very special surprise happened to me." Her mother was all ears. "I met Raju, and we reconnected." Her mother was surprised, happy, and worried at the same moment. Januma was overjoyed when Sumi told her that Raju was willing to wait and would help her to convince her father.

And for the next few days, Sumi's mom had to nudge her daughter to bring back from her fantasy world.

A darling daughter is a reflection of her
mother.
The lineage of love forever she prolongs.
Her laughs and cries are the stimulating
sounds.

*A vivacious daughter keeps the home
pulsating around.*

She was listening to the breathing of the sleeping
nature. She was in her dreamy delirium—the ecstasy
of love. Sumi was awakened gently by a devotional
sound. She listened to her mother's prayer to the
rising sun in the pink sky. She saw the old walls and
the dreary surroundings with the eyes of a poet. The
house and the universe seemed magical. The softly
singing wind had been blowing from one mountain
top to another for some time.

She got up to embrace and indulge the special
moments. That included checking the mail for Raju's
letter before anyone got hold of it. In the last four
months, they had exchanged countless verses on
paper and through the rare phone call, even though
they both were extremely busy. Sumi was stretching
her minutes to the extent that they could snap
sometimes. The wedding of Shan with Sona was
looming around the corner.

Almost a week before their wedding day, the red
canopy was stretched from one end to the other,
covering the whole front yard. Sumi's father was
giving orders to the workers to put yellow-and-green
borders with the fancy decorations on the mandap.
The actual wedding ceremony would be at the bride's
house. But the groom's house needed all the elegance
for the Lord Ganesh's adoration and for the reception

of the newlyweds. It was as tastefully done as her family could afford.

When they were making the guest list, Sumi had mentioned the Mody family in Vadodara to be included on the invitation list. But her father rejected it in one word, *no*, without looking in her direction. Her father might have noticed some letters coming to Sumi but did not inquire about them for some mysterious reason of his own.

Two days before the wedding, an unplanned get-together occurred. First, Sona's brothers came with some gifts for the groom. Sumi's cousin arrived and went to talk to her parents in the back room. Shortly afterward, one elderly couple and their son, named Vasant, arrived. Sumi's parents were very welcoming to them. The lady was closely staring at Sumi when she was serving them tea and snacks.

The lady suggested Sumi to come and sit next to her. "I understand that you will finish your PhD soon?" she asked Sumi.

"I have several months more," Sumi replied, withholding her usual charm. After a few such questions, the purpose of their visit was loud and clear.

Her mamu stopped by and joined in the chitchat. Looking at Sona's brothers, he said, "Some of you know my friend Sam Mody and his son Raju? Raju's research paper has made a big impact in the science community of biophysics. He just heard from a university in California...I forget which one!"

"Stanford University," Sumi chirped in.

All eyes turned toward her. Her father was glaring, and her mother was uncomfortable. Vasant's eyes narrowed with the suspense—around the name, Raju. Sumi slipped away to hide behind the door. And the topic of conversation was swiftly changed. But at that point, Sumi's father realized that her mamu was the mastermind behind the Raju-saga.

Priya had come alone to attend the wedding. On the day of the wedding, she helped Sumi with her hair and makeup. Since she had lived in the big city of Mumbai, Priya considered herself an expert in the fashion world.

"You just wait and see how glamorous you will look after I am done with my artwork." Priya artistically styled and adorned Sumi's hair with the strings of fresh flowers. Wrapped in a deep green silk sari with the golden thread embroideries, Sumi looked gorgeous.

"You know whom I wish could see me today?" Sumi said. Priya gave her an understanding look and a light kiss on her cheek.

If it is a day,
you come as sunshine and glance over me.
If it is a night,
you come as a moon and gleam over me.

A sad cloud covered her pretty face as she missed Raju.

"Did you see that? My father invited this Vasant guy to spoil my mood? I feel so weird when he stares at me. His father is a famous lawyer, and Vasant is a partner in their family law firm. Now…how am I going to conjure up an excuse and say, 'Thanks, but no thanks'?" Sumi whined to her friend.

To distract her, Priya asked, "Is Anu coming?"

"Yes. She is joining us at the wedding venue. She is bringing a friend but has been very secretive about him. She told me only his name, Binu. Well, we will find out soon." Excited, both friends went to check on the groom.

Sumi knocked on the door, and her brother opened it. He was wearing a long royal blue silk jacket, called a sherwani, and a turban with a small crown on his head. Sumi was overwhelmed with emotions.

Her brother was three years older, but he had always treated Sumi like a friend. Their childhood flashed across her eyes: the skinny boy playing the sword game with her. When Sumi would be defeated in the board games, he used to take her frustrated sisterly beatings with a laugh, the little boy running to be first everywhere, and nowhere! She also remembered him coming home, triumphant and filling up the cupboard with the trophies.

"Oh! You look so handsome." Her voice choked.

She picked up a decorated tray and applied a kumkum tilak with the third finger of her right hand. It is an auspicious custom in Hinduism to put a red mark on the forehead as a good luck symbol. Every ritual is as precious as the vibrations of the giver and the receiver. Sumi tied a red thread around his right wrist and wished a protective aura around her brother.

"Thank you, sis. Your loving aspiration is my biggest strength. I am a bit nervous today. Stay close to me," he said. His two friends and Priya intervened before the room got heavier with sentiments.

The groom's party arrived at the bride's home. The atmosphere was lively with the drums and clarion. The young crowd was dancing. Finally, the bride's party came out and put garlands to welcome the groom's party. The mother of the bride ceremoniously welcomed the groom.

In that joyful hoopla, Sumi noticed Ajay! And right behind him…Raju! They both had lined up to welcome the guests with the host family and friends. Sumi could not believe her eyes. Raju was staring at Sumi with playful adoration. She got so distracted that her brother had to pull her arm to walk with him. Sumi's mom followed her gaze and noticed Raju. Again, mixed feelings came over her about the situation concerning an intercaste marriage and her beloved daughter.

Sumi couldn't wait to find out how they managed to come! She whispered the question to her brother, and he replied, "I was just telling to Sona that you wanted to send the invitation, but our father had refused. So she invited them…Are you happy now?" He gave her a kind smile.

The bride arrived, dressed in a white-and-red silk sari, delicately escorted by her maternal uncle. Her head was covered with the red sheer sari presented by the groom's family. Sona, adorned in fine jewelry and makeup, looked very beautiful. All admiring eyes were on her face. Sumi nudged her brother to blink and show some modesty. Sona sat next to the groom in the royal chair, and the priest started chanting the holy mantras.

As the scriptures say, "The wedding ceremony signifies the purifying of the mind, body, and soul of the bride and groom."

Sona's parents came forward for kanyadan. "During kanyadan, the bride's parents give their daughter away in marriage. The groom makes three promises: to be just (dharma), earn sufficiently to support his family (artha), and love his wife (kama). He repeats these vows thrice in the presence of Agni (the sacred fire) and all who are gathered there. The bride's parents place her right hand into the hand of the groom and place their left hands underneath. Betel nut, flowers, and fruit with gold are placed on the couple's hands, signifying blessings and prosperity…In the second part of the ceremony, the bride and groom circumambulate the holy fire four times. The bride and groom take seven steps while seven blessings are spoken in Sanskrit. The groom puts the red kumkum powder on the bride's forehead and a mangalsutra, a gold-and-black-beaded necklace around her neck. The kumkum and the mangalsutra are the most precious symbols for a married woman, as the ring is in Western culture."

After the priest declared them as husband and wife, the newlyweds went to the elders for salutation. Sumi had to guide them so no elder relative would be forgotten. Otherwise, there could be a little uproar and complaints!

Sumi gave a warm hug to welcome her older brother's wife, now called Bhabhi, and thanked her at the first opportunity she got. "Sonabhabhi, you already won me over by inviting someone."

Sona gave her a mischievous smile. "I know. Now go to him. We will manage without you."

Sumi quietly stepped back and proceeded to meet one anxiously waiting guest. Raju's brother Ajay had disappeared with his friends.

"What an unexpected pleasure! I wouldn't ask you how you managed to come, but you made my day unbelievably special," Sumi whispered in his ear…

Later, her friend Priya told Sumi that Vasant had been intensely watching them. Priya said, laughing, "You were standing so close to Raju. I am sure he must have been tempted to put his arms around you."

"Oh, it was so noisy." Sumi tried to give a lame excuse, which was drowned in the laughter.

Anu had come late and was sitting at the far end of the banquet hall. Sumi went to greet her, with Raju by her side. Anu's companion Binu seemed familiar to Sumi, but there was no time to talk about it. Anu had planned to stay in town for the next few days. At the moment, both girlfriends were overjoyed to meet each other.

The dinner arrangements were artistically elegant. Sona's close relatives were dressed in the traditional yellow-colored outfits to serve food. The guests sat on the soft pillows, and the plates were lined up in front of them on the decorated low stools. The large round plates were filled with several savory and sweet items. The groom's family had to sit in a special order, according to their relationship to the groom. The bride and groom took the center seats. Next to the bride, only her sister and one friend would sit, followed by the guests. Sumi took her place next to her brother and then her parents and other relatives. The host family sincerely kept a close watch on the needs of their guests.

Sona's father did not believe in extravagance, so the gifts were exchanged quietly. The moment of smile in tears arrived. The bride's parents' and siblings' eyes were filled with tears as they walked with their beloved daughter up to the gate. They helped her to sit next to her prince in the decorated white horse carriage. They were separating from a piece of their hearts. Their little girl had become a charming woman and was going to her husband's house forever.

The bud of our meadow will bloom in your garden.
The bird of our nest will sing on your crest.
Our love and joy are wrapped in her.
Please take care of our darling daughter.

Sona might have been given advice from her mother, something like, "This is a big occasion when the bride enters her new home. This is quite daunting for the bride as she doesn't know what to expect. The household rhythm, systems, and arrangement are totally new. The best tactic is to be traditionally dressed and speak when spoken to. Always use your right hand for pujas and rituals. Praying to Lord Rama and Sita are considered auspicious on this occasion."

Flutter of Wings

The melodious tunes of the shehnai enhanced the joyous, auspicious, and welcoming occasion at the groom's house. Sumi's mother was waiting at the door, holding a silver dish containing a small earthen lamp, a diya, flowers, and red kumkum. Mother welcomed her new daughter.

This relationship would be very much intertwined in a joint family life. So both women tried their best to start off on the right foot. The next custom followed: Sumi detained the groom and bride at the door until her brother gave her a gift. The humorous and witty comments flew around from the relatives, everyone encouraging her to raise the demand. Finally, Sumi welcomed them in after receiving some cash from Shan.

Just inside the door, the bride delicately nudged a pot of rice and coins, symbols of fertility and prosperity. Then the bride and groom played a game of finding a ring from the vessel of milk—an excuse to touch each other's fingers. These age-old customs set the tone for long-lasting conjugal bliss that includes all the members of the clan.

Every member of the family had some role to play during the wedding ceremony. The noise, commotion, disorder, and children were the natural lively elements of the wedding scenario. In Sumi's house, the serene silence of the night was welcomed after the two days of excitement. The newlyweds happily scurried away to their pink-petals-and-satin-smooth bed.

Sumi and her cousin Risa stayed up, talking until midnight. Risa had come for two days and had to leave right after breakfast the next morning. Sumi's uncle came to take her to the airport. Sumi, Sona, and Shan accompanied her. Sona looked beautiful with her long braided hair adorned with diamond pins—wearing a red silk sari and red glass bangles.

When their uncle took a turn in the other direction, Shan was surprised. "Hey, Mamu! Why do we go this way?"

"Ask your sister." Their uncle chuckled. Shan looked at Sumi. She blushed and then shyly said, "While you drop off Risa, I am going to spend that hour with Raju. He is leaving by tonight's train. Risa knows about it." Risa nodded in agreement. Sumi wouldn't have dared to plan this meeting with Raju on the day of the reception at their house. But this wonderful excuse made this encounter possible. Sumi's uncle was more than happy to accommodate the lovebirds.

The car stopped at the city park. Sumi got out and waved, saying, "See you in an hour," and hurried toward Raju, who was waiting under the arc of the garden's gate. They went hand in hand and sat under the gulmahor tree. The vibrant red flowers and bright green foliage made it an exceptionally striking sight, the true expression of their mood at the time. The early morning sun was playfully peeking through the screen of the leaves, giving them the illusion they were in their own private world.

His simple touch sent thousands of tremors through her body. Raju said to Sumi, "It feels like it has been ages since our sweet interlude on the train. Yesterday, I saw my beautiful lady in a way I hadn't seen her before, and it was wonderful. The delicate peacocks on your sari, the white strands of flowers on your hair, and that crimson lipstick on the petals of your lips…Wow! That smile robbed me completely."

"When I saw you there, my soul slipped away from me. You were a total distraction for me. I don't think I was very attentive to other people afterward…and I was scolded for that." Sumi gaily complained.

"Did your father recognize me?" Raju inquired.

"No, but he asked my mother about my disappearance right after the wedding ceremony! You are coming for the reception tonight, right? Please, try to talk to him," Sumi requested.

"I will try my best. Wish me luck. But first I have to discuss a few important issues with you. One is, I have an offer to go to the USA for two to three years to further my research. I want your input about it."

Sumi waited as Raju paused for a few moments to organize his thoughts. Eventually, his sincere, gentle words floated in the air. "I hope we can make some definite plans about our wedding, Sumi. Consider this a marriage proposal." Raju looked in Sumi's eyes, his voice full of hopes and dreams.

Sumi gazed intently in his eyes to make sure that she was not dreaming. Hearing those exhilarating words, she was spellbound. The stillness enveloped them. She heard only the whispers of her inner voice in the blissful silence. Her soul was singing…"Take my hand. Take my whole life too…"

Sumi's answer was written all over her face, and her beloved read her reply with delight. He held her in a heavenly embrace. Sumi knew that she did not want to be anywhere else but there in his arms. His sweet lips were unfolding like a soft rose, and her face resembled the sun-kissed petals of a lily. Their souls were soaring on the wings of an eagle.

"Someone loves me! I found the joy none other like this before. I am dying with these strange sensations, but I never felt so alive before." She was reflecting the true and pure ecstasy, and time stood by to let their feelings flow.

The tantalizing tunes are gently repeating.
A secret song of love her heart is reciting.

The buds are blooming and the birds are
cooing.
The buzz all around hums; he is pursuing!

The trickling of scarlet petals from the gulmahor tree brought them back to earth. They talked and planned briefly about how and when to get married.

"You know what? When I told my parents and Ajay about our chance meeting on the train, they pestered me with so…many questions! My parents are quite excited and have started remodeling our house with your image in mind," Raju said.

Sumi was absolutely charmed by her beau.

"And one more person is pulling for you—my cousin Nina. She was one year junior to you in the postgraduate program in Vadodara, and you choreographed the folk dance for their department's annual day function," Raju continued.

"Oh, yes. I remember that sweet girl, Nina," Sumi said.

The hour was too short to remember, and the moments were too profound to forget. To sentimental hearts, nothing and yet everything made sense.

On the way home, in her uncle's car, Sumi was quiet. She had yet to know her new sister-in-law well enough to share her secrets. Her brother asked a few questions and then moved on to talk about the important event of that evening.

It was a very special evening for Shan and Sona. The bride, groom, and all the houseguests were ready to receive their honorable guests. The reception was in full swing. A small stage was decorated where Sumi's parents, the groom, and the bride were standing. And next to them, the bride's parents were in the receiving line. The guests would go on to the stage to congratulate the newlyweds and would be introduced to the family members. Sumi and her cousins were directing them toward the food area to mingle with other people.

After some time, Raju and Ajay arrived with Sona's brothers. As soon she saw Raju, Sumi told Priya, "Here I go again. I won't be able to focus on my sisterly duties. Keep an eye on me in case I do anything silly."

Earlier, Sumi had told Priya briefly about her dreamy morning with Raju. Priya had cheerily responded, "You lucky, lucky girl. I am jealous of you. Now do not let him get away, okay?" Sumi had wanted to discuss it first with her mother, but since Priya was leaving right after the reception, she told her first.

At one point in the evening, when Sumi's father sat down to take a break, Raju went to talk to him. But after two or three short sentences, her father rose and walked away. Maybe he felt awkward talking with the young scientist, or maybe his dislike overtook him.

The guests were clustered in groups. On one side, Sumi and Shan's friends were laughing and having a good time. Raju and Ajay were in the center of the group. Anu, Priya, and several other friends were talking loudly over the sound of the music. Sumi along with her mamu and his daughter Kim joined the group to get in on the fun.

Sumi had overlooked that, not too far from them, her father and relatives were talking to Vasant and his parents. She had forgotten the one-sided conversation earlier she had had with her father. When her father found her alone, he had said, "Sumi! Vasant is a good candidate, and I don't see any reason to say no to him. I am going to talk to his parents. And we should decide something positively before they leave tonight." Before Sumi could say anything, many people had entered the room, and his words were left hanging behind, back in the house.

The evening function was nearly over, and most of the guests were gone. Sumi and Raju were standing side by side with her mamu and their friends, joking and laughing, which drew everyone's attention. Then Sumi heard her father's commanding voice, "Sumi! Please come here." She recognized the subtle, suppressed anger in that one short sentence. She went over and said hello to the group. Her father continued talking to Vasant's parents, "So, as I was saying, you are agreeable, and now everything depends on what Vasant…"

"Excuse me, can I talk to Vasant for a minute?" Sumi firmly spoke. She turned and walked away as Vasant followed.

"You seem like a very nice person, but I am sorry. Please say no for me. I am engaged to someone," she earnestly said, and she glanced at Raju. All were looking at them even though they could not hear what she was saying. Vasant's face turned from surprise to fury in several seconds.

Vasant marched back, huffing to his parents, and said, "I don't see any reason to stay here any longer. Let's go." His confused parents exchanged a few words of courtesy and followed their son. Sumi's father looked helplessly at his brother who ran after the guests and profusely apologized. Sumi was afraid to look at her parents. Her father could not endure the puzzled looks on the faces of his guests.

After one irate look at Sumi, he started to walk away. She felt the vibrations of anger as he passed by her and went toward stock-still Raju. Her mamu came with the quick pace and stopped him by gently grabbing his arm. He whispered to Sumi's father, "Mohanbhai, calm down…"

Her father glared at Raju and then Sumi. "Did you see what that girl did to my guests? I know the reason behind her crude behavior."

He turned his gaze toward Mamu. "You have no right to misguide my daughter like this." As her father's low-toned voice resonated, everyone froze, as did the tears in Sumi's eyes. Again, she heard her father's firm voice. "You ask him to leave…before I say something insulting."

Most of them knew whom he wanted out of his house. He freed his arm and disappeared inside the house to be away from everyone, including his wife.

Januma could not believe what had happened in those last few minutes. She shook herself out of that shock and went to Raju. She apologized and kindly thanked him for attending Shan's wedding. At the moment, the best thing for Raju to do was to leave.

But before going, Raju walked to where Sumi was standing, full of regrets and embarrassments. He clasped her hands and said, "So long. I am leaving now but to come back soon. No more tears in these beautiful eyes—a smile for me!"

Sumi forgot all her sad thoughts, gave him a fresh flowery smile and a gentle hug, and said, "See you soon. I promise." Silent sorrow was beating in her chest.

Raju respectfully joined his palms and bowed his head to say, "Namaste," to Sumi's mom and other elders before walking away. He seemed solemn but unshaken, dignified but humble.

Sumi went to Ajay and very kindly said, "Little brother! Thanks for coming. Have a safe journey and convey my regards to your mom and papa." Shan and Sona thanked both the brothers and presented a beautiful box of sweets.

Mamu and all their friends walked with Raju and Ajay to the gate and beyond. Forlorn, Sumi's eyes followed him.

He walks away to come closer to my heart.
He leaves, and I stay, but our souls do not
part.

Sumi could not recognize her own feelings, so she searched her brother's eyes. The gentle soul was torn between his new bride and the family drama. He chose to turn to his bride, who looked like a scared dove. Januma led Sumi inside the house.

Repercussions

The aftermath of the showdown at the reception appeared in different forms with different people. The silence for the first few hours was too thick. But they all pushed their disappointments aside to make the bride feel welcome. Sona needed some conventional environment to feel at home.

After a couple of days, Sumi stopped by her uncle's house on the way to the market. Mamu looked at her with a steady gaze and asked, "Do you want to marry Raju?"

"Yes." The direct question got a direct reply.

"Okay, first thing first. I will talk to your father and clarify the matter, one way or the other. It is agonizing to muddle in the middle," Mamu said.

"Sona will be gone to her mother's home tomorrow. That would be a proper time to talk with my papa." Her uncle agreed and planned to go to Sumi's house the next day.

The late morning assembly at Sumi's house was thumping with timorous expectations. The confrontation between Sumi's father and her uncle was agonizing. Her uncle's contribution in the initiation of this relationship was severely criticized by her father.

Januma addressed her husband. "There always has been a gap in yours, mine, and the children's thinking. We should not forget that they are respectful enough to ask for your permission." That statement reflected deep down bitterness in her, and Sumi felt like she was pushed into the dark well of the past.

After a heated exchange, her uncle was assertive. "But, Mohanbhai, why can't you see that they are made for each other? We all believe that marriages are made in heaven, right? I was only an instrument in their meeting. This relationship is beyond yours or my control. This young generation will forge ahead no matter what! It would be wise to recognize our good fortune that she is falling for a good boy like Raju. I can vouch for his nice family. We should count our blessings." Sumi was anxiously waiting for her father's response.

Finally, he spoke, "If this generation would do whatever they want to…then count me out." He got up and walked out through the front door. Sumi knew his usual style. Whenever upset, he would go out of the house and walk for a long time. Thinking how unhappy he would be, Sumi felt choked with emotions, and tears swelled up in her eyes. The most delicate bond was getting too thin to the point that it might break! Sumi, a loving daughter, would not be able to endure it.

A little girl in her asks the woman,
"Is this worth it?"
Her mind turns round and asks her heart,
"How can you bear it?"

She wanted to be alone, away from that situation, from those vibrations, and from her loved ones. She ran into the backyard and sat near the rosebush. It took several minutes to dry her tears.

She was lost in thought and had forgotten that Anu was to come. Sumi saw Anu standing in the back doorway. She hurriedly got up to greet her.

"Glad you are here. Where is Binu?" Sumi said.

"He is spending some time with his old neighbors." Anu's answer reminded Sumi of something.

"Oh! He is that Muslim boy Bashir! I remember his family moved to Delhi several years ago from this area. Wow! Tell me how did you reconnect with him?"

"I am here to tell you all about it."

It was close to lunchtime, so Sumi said, "Let's go out somewhere. I am anxious to get out of the house." Sumi informed her mother about their outing, and both friends went to a quiet family restaurant.

Anu was still quite emotionally perturbed about her broken marriage. The last three years had been challenging for her, and the grief had left deep marks on her charming face. Her once smiling eyes were sunken and glazed with sorrow and pain today. Her trembling voice recited her story.

"Sumi! Do you remember when you visited us in Kullu you asked me where RK was going in the middle of the day and I did not have an answer? You must have observed that the communication between us was very superficial. Our lives together were stagnant. I started to keep myself occupied with my studies. By the way, I am so grateful for your suggestion about revitalizing my dream to become an officer—adding a flower in the bouquet of my life,'" she mimicked Sumi.

"You are very welcome. When you are in the whirl of water, you may not see the shore, but, as a friend, it was my duty to guide you to the shore," Sumi replied. The waiter served samosas, their favorite appetizer.

"You know, samosas remind me of that year-end party at the military base in the Kullu. I was very excited about the opportunity to get dressed up and go out with my husband, something different from my usual dull routine. RK in a red shirt and me in black sari, I thought we looked like an elegant pair. I was meeting so many new officers and their wives for the first time.

"I was mingling with ladies, and I overheard, 'Hey! You see that man in the red shirt and the other guy standing next to him? I was told that they are a couple of homos. One guy has a lovely wife. I feel pity for her.' I was stunned as if somebody had slapped me across my face. I felt the whole world knew about this ugly secret except me."

Sumi was shocked to hear it. Seeing her friend in distress, she told Anu, "Please don't say any more. It is hurting you too much."

Anu composed herself and said, "Sumi! Actually for the first time, I am talking about those days in details...and maybe for the last. I want to put this grief in front of me and be aware of it so it does not creep up on me unexpectedly and make me miserable. Now I can see how naïve, submissive, and fearful a person I was. Wouldn't you think, as a wife, I would have some instinct about RK's behavior? But I did not want to face the reality for almost a year!"

"Yes. You have suffered long enough. Now is the time to tackle life head-on. And I can see that Binu is with you to protect you."

A bud in her prime was solemnly deprived.
Without a caring keeper, would have dried.
But in misty monsoon cloud,
she opened and survived.
The spring has arrived; her hope has
revived.

Anu continued, "Binu had kept in touch with my family since the high school years. But in the last two years, I would have broken into pieces without his love and support. He taught me to look beyond the half-full cup, to see life as a pitcher of happiness filled with good karma. With my inner strength and my well-wishers' support, I can replenish the cup of my life and move forward.

"Because he is a Muslim, there was some controversy amongst my relatives, but I don't care.

"When I was drowning in my socially perfect marriage, no one came to rescue me. My family, including my grandma, has given me their blessings, so that is all that matters. Okay, enough about me. Tell me, why did I see this lovely face so sad when I arrived at your house?"

Sumi told Anu briefly what had happened that morning. Anu said, "First of all, I want to tell you about your terrific conduct on the night of Shan's reception. Oh my stars! I saw a glowing example of one determined girl. You could not have talked the way you did with Vasant without a clear vision. Your energy was totally aligned with your intuition.

"In my opinion, Raju is the right choice for you. And from now onward, do not invest your precious time and energy in vacillation. Your father has the right to express his opinion, but he should not be given authority to design your life…You are a wise person and may take every step with open eyes. That Raju's family welcomes you is a very big plus point under the circumstances. Some of the problems seem overwhelming, but you can handle it. You are strong."

Sumi was delighted to hear such a clear analysis. She felt no more agitation, just a joyful peace of mind. Sumi said, "Now I see the big picture of my future in the proper perspective. From now on, Raju will have an undistracted companion, a woman without the ghost of a little girl attached to her. Okay, my friend! You have helped me see the lighted path. I will amble, not tremble."

The bright smiles and beaming eyes sent pleasant vibes all around. The lunch was over. Both friends got up, hugged, and proceeded to face the world.

It was early evening. Right after dinner, Sumi's father had gone to his brother's house, and Shan had gone to pick up Sona. Mother and daughter huddled up to talk. Sumi's mother asked, "You may start from that morning when you all had gone to the airport with Risa. I know where you were headed, you sneaky one!"

"Oh! It was an eventful morning. You will be shocked to hear this. Raju asked me to marry him, and I said yes. Sorry, Ma, I had no time to consult with you." Sumi hugged her mother as Januma wiped tears from her eyes with a corner of her cotton sari.

"I am glad and proud. Now I know why you had to clarify the situation without any further delay at the reception. That's what I would expect from my daughter—to be fearless and truthful. And, sweetheart! You will have to be prepared to deal with the consequences when you go against the flow." Her mother's wisdom and confidence made Sumi feel stronger.

Januma impartially said, "If there would have been any problem with your young man, I would have stood by your father, but not for this caste objection. No, I will not support him. And this is not the first time I am defying him. I have done so several times before." Her mother's words reminded her of Maa Durga, the goddess of power behind the work of creation, preservation, and destruction of the world. The name *Durga* in Sanskrit means "invincible." The syllable *du* is synonymous with the four devils of poverty, sufferings, famine, and evil habits. The *r* refers to diseases, and the *ga* is the destroyer of sins, injustice, irreligion, cruelty, and laziness.

Sumi prayed a salutation to Maa Durga.

Sumi contemplated for a while about how to ask about her deep down trepidations. "Mom, after all the struggles, what if I do not get along with Raju and his family? What is the guarantee?"

"Honey, marriage is an institution. You enter into it with dreams, but you have to be awake and aware to make them come true. The intimate and complicated relationship between a husband and wife will bring shades of fondness, friendship, love, expectations, and disappointments invariably.

"But the most important pillars are you and him, the core of this relationship. If you are set to deal with your spouse in action-reaction mode, then failure will not be too far off. I think a woman has to give more and expect less. Patience is a virtue, absolutely required for your spiritual growth."

And moreover, don't try to rush relationships;
for the cup to run over, it must first be filled.

Sumi's mother continued, lost in deep thoughts, "A long-lasting relationship is based on love, care, tolerance, sacrifice, and devotion. Loyalty has to come from both sides. I think one has to figure out within a reasonable time that your partner is worth the efforts or not. We do not want to waste this precious life for a lost cause."

Sumi dreamily spoke, "I feel Raju is right for me. Every time I have analyzed my thoughts, the same positive echo resonates in my spirit. I cannot imagine my life without him."

Januma's passionate voice was fervent with emotions. "This is what I was waiting to hear.

"O my love! You are ready to sail, and you have my blessings."

Mother asked, "What word comes to your mind when you think of marriage and Raju?"

And her daughter replied, "The word that comes to me is—*devotion*."

In her own serene sky, she flies like a seagull.
She is prepared and eager; her flight should be regal.

She will share with her mate true sentient
sight.
An unassuming ego and the path will be
bright.

As they heard footsteps, they went to the front room to welcome Sona. Now it was Shan and Sona's turn to hear Sumi's story, and her brother did a dance of joy.

Sumi went back to work and decided to finish her thesis as fast as she could. She worked with added energy and enthusiasm. Two more months of hard work paid off, and her thesis was complete. She kept herself away from Minu and the ladies' group at work. She was preoccupied with daydreams. The realization that she would be going far away from that place made her more aloof.

Her Own Serene Sky

It had been almost three months since Shan and Sona's wedding. For the newlyweds, that time was quite short, but to the separated lovebirds, it was unbearably long. Sumi and Raju missed each other terribly. There was no more discussion about Sumi's marriage in her home. The usual pleasant interaction continued between father and daughter in the presence of the new member in the family, Sona.

Raju reminded Sumi often to set the wedding date. Sumi realized that the time had come to be honest and let the family know about their future plans. She knew that the news of her going away would be hard on her family.

"Ma, Raju got the confirmation. He is invited to continue his research project in the USA. We will be going to America next year, in January—only for two to three years." Sumi hesitantly said.

"Well, I am being tested by you young people. I am constantly relearning how to let go of my son and my daughter. I am repeating the prayer I used to say when you were little: 'God, grant me patience, but hurry!' with a deep, different connotation. When butterflies are ready to fly out of their cocoons, no one can stop them, but at the same time, we can be the flowers for you to come back," Januma sadly said.

In the month of September, when the fury of summer disappeared behind the monsoon clouds and before the misery of winter cold could set in, Sumi was ready to invite the unseasonable spring in her life. She was wondering how to talk to her uncle and other family members about the secret mission. And, as if nature wanted to help, her father went out of town for a couple of days. Sumi called a family meeting.

Sumi's mamu occupied the big chair like a ring leader, and the members of the "team" sat around on the floor. Sumi's cousin Kim was ready with paper and pen to jot down the minutes. Sona had been very supportive to Sumi all those months and proved to be totally trustworthy. Shan was cautiously enthusiastic. He had talked with his father-in-law and was encouraged by his positive support.

Her mother kept herself at a distance from the group. Januma was feeling guilty for conspiring behind her husband's back. And her heart was quivering with the thought of trusting some stranger with her daughter. The lines of worry were making her graceful face look older.

"I have to defend my thesis next week. After that, hopefully I will be free. I am considering having the wedding on the third Thursday of September!" Sumi said.

Everyone had different questions regarding how and where this secret event could be accomplished. "Raju has consented to my plan that he will come to our town, and we will quietly get married. After the ceremony, we will inform Papa. Mamu has to find a safe wedding venue. Could Shan and Sona be in the welcoming committee?"

"I am including my name in that committee. And I propose that Rajubhai and party stay at our house," Kim jumped in.

Mamu laughed. "I was wondering how she kept quiet for a full ten minutes!"

Kim, four years younger than Sumi, had been a dancing shadow to her older cousin since her childhood. Kim had a bubbly personality, laughing and crying in the same sentence. She was the one who had blurted out years ago, "Sumi! You should elope with Raju." But, at that time, Sumi had replied very emotionally, "I would never do that."

Remembering that conversation, Sumi smiled.

"I have learned my lesson: never say never again… right, Kim? See! I am doing exactly what you had told me to do." For sure, her mother heard the subtle sadness in Sumi's voice.

After getting confirmation about the wedding date from Raju, the plans were finalized. He wrote that his best friend, and Ajay would come with him. Sumi thought that a girl's presence would be good. So upon her request, his cousin Nina was invited.

One morning, Sumi and Sona were on their way to purchase a bridal sari and other required items. As per tradition, the shopping event before the wedding is considered very auspicious, when the bride-to-be and her parents go to purchase many exclusive items for the upcoming wedding.

They ran into her uncle, who noticed no excitement or joy on Sumi's face. Her mamu said, "I have selected the venue for your wedding. I will give you details later…So why this sad face?"

"We are going to purchase the wedding accessories. So, naturally, sister is distressed to be doing it secretly," Sona said sympathetically.

Mamu put his hand on Sumi's head and spoke kindly, "We tried our best to convince your papa, and we will keep on trying to make peace in the family. But for now, my dear, be brave!" Sumi hugged her uncle warmly. Those two words she would treasure her whole life.

"Be brave, be honest, and remain true to your soul."

Sumi purchased very few things for herself, but a nice sari for her mother-in-law and some gifts for other family members. Sumi's last night as a bachelorette in her home was wistful. Every step had become emotive, and her mind a war zone. The irony was, Sumi wanted to run away, but never leave. She knew that she would never forget the tantalizing twist in her heart and mind.

Before she went in her bedroom, Januma told her gently, "My dear, I don't know how to put my feelings into words. You have been such a joy in my life, and, at times, my lifeline to swim and survive. This home will always be open for you. So never fear. Do not let anyone suffocate the flicker flame of your spirit. You are a noble soul. Be kind and generous. Allow love to flow freely."

The vibrations of the blessed words made Sumi feel very precious. The deep love and understanding between the mother and her daughter were genuine, like the fragrance in a flower. That helped her to calm down. The weight of the secret felt heavy but sweet and tingling.

Wildflowers Wonder

It seemed like a usual Thursday morning in Januma's house. But in her mind, it was not much less than a wrenching day. The whacks of the world and the concerns of her children had turned the one-time pillar of strength into an insecure mom. She sighed, "Oh! God! How strange are love's ways. The eyes of lovers embrace, but the family ties snap."

Sumi came out of the house around nine o'clock in the morning. Her father was working in the front yard. He looked up, wished her a good day at work, and got busy with his task. Sumi stood there for a few moments, bade him, "Namaste," silently, and slowly walked out of the gate...Sona followed her with a small suitcase after five minutes. They hired a rickshaw and proceeded to the wedding destination.

Shan, his friend, mamu, Kim, and Sona's father were waiting near the gate of the Enchanted Ashram. The place was in a quiet area of the town, and from the outside, it looked like an untamed jungle. Sumi was pleasantly surprised when she went inside. The lush green trees were overhanging the herb gardens as far as she could see. The butterflies, peacocks, and rabbits were fearlessly roaming.

"But where is my prince?" Sumi wondered. Sumi gave a worried look to Shan.

He laughed and said, "Don't worry. The groom's party is waiting at the 'Circle of Spirits.'"

Sona and Sumi were led into a room for Sumi to get ready. Sumi had purchased an inexpensive cotton-silk sari and had painted an artistic border. It had taken half the night for her to finish the border of that six-yard sari. But her creative self wouldn't have it any other way. She was also wearing some simple gold jewelry.

The groom was anxiously waiting. He was attractively dressed in a maroon gold-thread-embroidered silk kurta over white pants. The Circle of Spirits was designed to be a focal point of the Ashram. The wedding ceremonies would be a rare event, but it was a regular place for the group meditation. The big circle was surrounded by mango and banyan trees.

The gentle music was playing. The fragrance of the orange blossoms was nostalgic. The pigeons and peacocks were playing around as if they owned the place. In the center of the circle, a priest was ready with the means and materials required for the wedding ceremony.

The music stopped. With the flow of the gentle breeze, they heard the gentle bells of her anklets. The bride came down the trail, which was lined with purple and yellow wildflowers.

Sumi's slow footsteps captured everyone's attention. The peacocks and the hummingbirds were mesmerized by the angelic bride...She was artistically wrapped in a white silk sari with maroon border. She had light makeup with red and white bindis over her eyebrows and one in the center of her forehead. Strings of white delicate flowers adorned her hair and rested on both shoulders. She looked like Mother Nature's divine daughter.

Shan, a proud brother, went to greet his sister. He held Sumi's hand and gently brought her near Raju. He presented his sister's hand as if he was giving away his most precious treasure. He couldn't speak; the words got caught in his throat. Shan's soft moist eyes expressed his overwhelming emotions.

Raju took Sumi's hand and tenderly squeezed. A woman helper brought two leis made of whisper pink plumeria flowers. The sweet fragrance filled the air as the bride and groom put the leis around each other's necks. The bride and groom took their assigned seats in the center of the Circle of Spirits. The priest was a very learned yogi of the Ashram. The priest's white hair and long beard reminded Sumi of her grandfather. A smile flickered as she thought, *I hope Bapa has kept up with me. Otherwise, he would not recognize me in this getup, from wherever he would be looking at me.*

The wedding ceremony was performed with Vedic hymns and holy mantras. Raju and Sumi had good knowledge of Sanskrit and were able to understand and appreciate all that was said.

"The love that is shared is a beautiful thing, which enriches the soul and makes the heart sing," the priest said. He asked the bride and groom to speak if they wished.

"My love for you is constant like a sunbeam on the smiling fields. My love for you has blossomed with the changing of the seasons. Our love joins tender minds, but it is knotted in our hearts. My love will continue to grow deeper as we walk hand in hand to the shimmering horizon and will melt to be one in the infinite neverland," Raju said.

"My heart is bursting with pride and joy as I promise to be your wife. We tie each other to be partners to help each other to liberate our souls and fly free. My love is like a gentle flowing river that would warmly touch every life connected to you. We both step out in this world with love and compassion in our hearts. We pray that through our journey, the joy we feel striving to reach our potentials will enlighten our path to find happiness within," Sumi said.

The wildflowers wonder why two lovers surrender!
The gentle petals sprinkle; the tender tears twinkle.
O bird of my soul! Don't be coy; come sing the song of joy.

The poem of my heart recites the lyrics of
true love.

The wedded couple and the guests joined
the Ashram's members in their prayer to the
Supreme Soul:

...I am!
From oneness and duality,
from opposites I am free.
From coming into being and ceasing to be
and from light I am free.
I shine!
I am pure and everlasting.
I am the eternal...

The fragrance of sandalwood filled the air. The
delighted birds sang, and the leaves clapped in
harmony as the bride and groom hugged and kissed
the small group of well-wishers. Raju's brother, Ajay,
was beside himself with joy. He hugged his brother
and his bhabhi tightly and then dashed out with a
friend to send a telegram to their parents, announcing
the completion of the wedding of Raju and Sumi.

The happy event was over, and Sumi was forced
to face the dreaded task of sending a message to her
father. Sumi took out a folded piece of paper and
handed it to Raju. He read,

Saryu Parikh

Dear Papa,

Raju and I got married this morning. We will
come to bow our heads at your feet and
pray for your blessings. I have faith in your
gentle love, and I know that your trust in me
will prevail.

Wherever I live in this world, I am your
daughter, and you are my papa.

With love and respect,
Sumi

Sumi looked at Raju with tear-filled eyes. That little note was going to hurt her father sharply. Raju put his arm around her shoulders and pulled her closer, an affirmation of his support and empathy. Sumi's mamu made arrangements to send the letter with her father's favorite nephew.

All the guests enjoyed the scrumptious meal served on banana leaves. The sweet, subtle romantic atmosphere was humming the melodious tunes. The intuitive feeling that something good had happened was overwhelming in Sumi's heart. She received similar vibrations from Raju and everyone present in the Ashram.

They arrived at mamu's house after a stop at the Maa Durga's temple. When they went to the guest room, they found Ajay was fast asleep on the sofa.

Raju chuckled. "Look at him. He must be so sleepy that he dozed off before even changing his clothes. Good thing he left the bed for us. Please come and relax."

Sumi sat next to Raju. The conversation was building the bridge to touch each other's hands, then play of his fingers with hers. He grasped her full hand and gently pulled her. Sumi's face came very close, and Raju kissed her lips. Her first kiss from a man—her man! Sumi felt the passionate pressure of his lips on hers. Her face turned rosy pink, and his eyes glazed over with desire. But right away, they were alert, remembering a mischievous third person sleeping in the room. Raju kissed her fingers as she wiped the lipstick from his lips. Sumi rested her head on Raju's shoulder and closed her eyes.

My dream is realized, my prince by my side.
O my heart! You pulsate with ecstasy.
Yet, parting from my roots fills me with sorrow,
so tenderly you throb with agony.

Tormented Affection

It was a pleasant Thursday morning for Sumi's father. He lovingly tended the mango trees in his yard. He saw Sumi going to her lab and felt proud to have such a bright daughter. After her, he saw Sona leaving, and he assumed that she might be going to see her parents.

For lunch, Januma served him a special meal with some specific delicacies. So Sumi's father teased, "What is the occasion? Is it your brother's birthday?" That's the way he often teased his wife. Januma just smiled and got busy with her tasks.

When he went to his room for his afternoon nap, his nephew brought him a letter from Sumi, stating, "Sumi and Raju were married." And his world turned upside down. He had suspicion, but for things to turn out like this...he did not anticipate. He sat alone for a while and realized that everyone else in the family was a part of this conspiracy, including his wife. The special lunch was for the celebration of their daughter's wedding, of which he was kept unaware!

When he heard his wife's footsteps, he closed the door, shutting her out. Januma anxiously waited for some time, which seemed like forever. And finally when he came out, he walked away with determined steps. He went in the backyard to the pond of water. He picked up the bucket, filled it with cold water, and poured it over his head, washing away tears and his anger with the water. Januma was horrified to see this symbolic gesture of pouring water upon oneself—as one would do for a dead loved one. Januma watched the disappointed, saddened father helplessly as he collected some money, a few items of clothing, and left home without a word.

Shan and his wife Sona returned to a very quiet home. Their mother's face had turned red from crying. But she smiled through tears when she heard about the lovely wedding of her beloved Sumi.

"Ma, this union of Sumi and Raju seemed so natural. The wedding ceremony was simple but classy. And we had organized a very nice luncheon for the wedding party. Would it be okay to bring them to our house, around four o'clock this afternoon?" Shan said.

Januma was apprehensive. "Son, I am worried sick about your papa. We do not know where your papa has gone! He had left soon after reading Sumi's letter. The news is going to spread like wildfire. You will see our house swarming with uninvited relatives and neighbors in no time," she said. They both had assumed that their father was in his room.

"What? Papa is not here?" Shan's question brought back tears to Januma's eyes.

Sona came and sat next to her mother-in-law, and very soothingly, she told her, "Mom! Do not worry. So far, so good about sister's wedding. Shan and my brothers will find Papa." Januma listened to her kind words and squeezed her hand gently in appreciation.

Shan went out looking for his father at his relatives' homes. But wherever he went, he had to relay the news of Sumi's wedding, even though his father was not there. Around four o'clock in the afternoon, Shan had to go to mamu's house to bring Sumi, Raju, Ajay, and their cousin Nina to his place. He went with a happy mask covering his face.

As soon as Sumi saw Shan, she anxiously asked, "How did Papa take my news? Did you talk to him? Why aren't you saying something?"

Shan hesitated, thought about what to say, and then said, "Listen! Things are under control. I have not talked to Papa yet. You will see him later and find out yourself. Now let's gather our guests and go home."

That much information was enough for Sumi to know that something was terribly wrong and Shan did not want to talk about it. The smiling face but quivering heart of Sumi couldn't wait to go home.

When they arrived at her parents' home, it was crowded with the curious and concerned supporters. Sumi was anxiously looking for the one face that used to be delighted by a mere glimpse of his little girl and showed worry lines with any smallest problem in his daughter's life. Her father was not there. A twinge intensified. Sumi was afraid that on her rosy face the dews of pain might show up any moment.

She went to Januma, and they hugged each other emotionally. The question in Sumi's eyes about her father was left unanswered. The new couple was openly scrutinized, especially Raju, who was quite uncomfortable. He was encircled by strangers and was being quizzed endlessly. Ajay intervened and kept them involved in funny conversations so his brother could slip away to Sumi. The tea and snacks were served to the guests, and they were encouraged to say quick good-byes by Sumi's cousins and friends.

After the guests were gone, behind the closed doors, Januma told Sumi and Raju how their father had left after receiving Sumi's note, omitting a few details. Sumi understood the exact meaning of the pouring of the water.

"We had planned to leave tonight, but we will stay," Raju said.

"Yes, we will wait..." She had many things to say, but words did not come out. She appreciated her husband's decision.

Januma and her family trembled, remembering an incident from a few months before. There had been a story in the newspaper about a father who lay down in front of an oncoming train because his daughter had brought shame to the family. At that time, Sumi's papa had sympathized with the dead father, saying "Poor man. What else could he do?" What if anything like that happened? It was unthinkable.

An hour passed. Finally, Sumi's cousin returned with some good news. "Uncle is at his friend's house but refused to come home. He inquired, and I told him that Sumi would be gone by tonight's train... After that, he did not say anything more." A wave of relief and the leaves on the mango tree fluttered again.

It was decided that Raju and Ajay would go back to mamu's house, and Sumi and Nina would stay at her mom's home for the night. Early the next morning, Sumi and Nina went to mamu's house and surprised everyone by cooking a hot breakfast—of course, prepared under her aunt's supervision. Raju and Sumi had been waiting on pins and needles for her father to come home. Finally, Shan showed up in the late afternoon. It was hard to read his face. He was obviously distressed.

"I went in the morning to bring papa home from his friend's house, but he was too upset to talk with me. But he eventually came home around two o'clock after a lot of persuasion by his friend. We all sat and talked and talked about the situation. He perceives Sumi's decision to get married secretly as an insult to him. He is quite angry at Mom too. He does not know that you both are still here, and I have come to pick you up," Shan said.

Sumi did not need to hear anything more. She had confidence in her love for her father. Many times in the past, no matter how angry he would be at Januma or Shan, Sumi had been a link to keep him connected with the family.

Pure love, a beam of light, doesn't need a mirror.
Pure love gives, creates, and simply surrenders.

When Sumi, Raju, and Ajay arrived with Shan at their house, a small group of men was talking in the front room, and ladies were in the back room, not too far from them. Shan, Raju, and Ajay went in and found seats in the men's group. Sumi looked at her father, who turned his head away. Sumi hesitated for a moment and then went in the back room to her mother.

"Papa, Raju wants to say something," Shan said. Raju joined his hands to say, "Namaste," but in return, he received a blank look.

"Papa! With utmost respect, I request you to accept my union with your daughter, Sumi…I promise that I will faithfully take care of her. We could not imagine our lives without each other, so we had to take this step, not to hurt yours or anyone's feelings," Raju said. Sumi was nervously standing by the door, intently listening.

Sumi's father gave him a blank look and said, "It is too little, too late. Since my family wants you here, I am leaving." And he prepared to walk out.

Shan stopped him near the door and said, "Please, Papa! Be angry at us, scold us, but do not leave." But he started to put on his shoes, ignoring his son's plea. As he turned and raised his foot to step out, he heard his little girl's voice,

"Bapu! Don't go!" Sumi ran and touched his feet softly in adoration. Moments passed. Her father's eyes filled with tears. His hand moved, slowly touching her head to bless his daughter. Raju came and stood next to Sumi. The soft lines on her father's face hardened again, and he turned toward the door to step out.

"Please, sir! Give us a few minutes, and let me explain," Raju begged.

Sumi stood up and said, "Please, Papa! After that, if you still want us to leave this house, we will." So, reluctantly, he returned to his seat.

"Sir, do you remember my grandfather? He was a Shastry Brahmin, a preacher and a scholar in this city. My mom was his only child," Raju said.

One time, Mamu had mentioned to Sumi's father about Mr. and Mrs. Mody's intercaste marriage. But he ignored it, saying, "A son is recognized only by the father's family name."

Raju continued cautiously, "Years ago, when he found out that my mother liked a non-Brahmin student in his Sunday school class, he was upset. But my grandfather took time to find out if the young man was worthy of his daughter or not. He checked his background, friend circle, and education. Then he met with his family. And eventually, he trusted my father enough to bless my parents' intercaste marriage…

"I am sure that he had to face the resentments of many people, but he gave more importance to the person her daughter was choosing rather than his caste. My grandfather loved my dad like a son until the day he died," Raju finished in a soft tone.

Ajay jumped in and said, "So, Uncle, as you see— we are half Brahmin." With that unexpected input, Sumi's father was startled, but then a quick little smile touched his mouth.

"Papa! You always admire people with true convictions, and that's what I see in Raju and his family. Now you have to decide. Do you trust Mom's, Shan's, and my judgment, or that of society?"

"You have often praised Sumi as 'our sensible child.' And I believe that our elders' blessings and her good fortune have brought Raju into her life," Januma said.

With a worried look, her father asked, "Sumi, dear! Are you sure…you have made the right choice? Is this what you want?"

Sumi's muffled voice confessed, "Yes, Papa! This is what I want. I know you want to see me happy, and there is no one else for me, except…" She was too shy to say his name.

"Okay, so be it. I hope that you will turn out to be right in your choice. And I wish that you do not suffer any consequence for stepping out of line of tradition."

Her father reluctantly put his right hand over Raju's head in acceptance of his son-in-law. Both newlyweds bowed their heads and cherished the moment, even though it had come halfheartedly. The cloud of affection warmed Januma's heart, as others wiped their teary eyes. Love prevailed, and they heard the melodious music from Lord Krishna's flute, resonating in their home.

Everyone happily settled down, and sweet murmurs filled the house. Sumi's father looked at his wife and spoke calmly, "We should have a puja and celebration tomorrow. What do you think, Shan?"

"Oh! Yes." Shan and Januma were overjoyed.

Sumi's father addressed his son-in-law with respect, in the traditional style. He said, "Beta Raju! Please extend our invitation to your honorable parents to come here tomorrow. We will not start the puja until they get here."

A neighbor offered to use their phone, so Sumi and Raju went to the neighbor's house to call his parents. His parents happily assured them that they would leave early in the morning by car and would arrive by midday tomorrow. Sumi and Raju felt as light as a feather. Sumi was talking, laughing, and dancing at the same time. It was a good thing that Raju was holding her hand to keep her close to him. Walking back from the neighbor's house, Sumi saw her uncle entering her house.

Pointing at him, Sumi told Raju, "My papa's older brother is the head of the family. He is tough and will give us a hard time, so be prepared."

They gave the information to Januma about Raju's parents' arrival plans and headed to her papa's room to face the final cordon of resistance. They were stunned outside the door to hear the conversation.

Her father's apologetic voice said, "But, brother! I protested as much as I could."

"I raised you and taught you everything after our parents died at a young age. You went ahead and accepted this intercaste marriage. Now who is going to marry my daughters?" his brother said.

"After all these years of sacrifices and services for you, if you still feel that I owe you the happiness of my daughter…then you are absolutely wrong. And, brother! I don't know much, but that much I understand that we are not that kind of people who clings to their hatred because they do not want to face their own fear and ignorance," Sumi's father spoke with agitated voice.

He paused for a while and then said, "It would be wise of you to be on my side and support my decision." Her father's firm voice was followed by a complete silence.

Sumi nudged Raju to enter the room. When they bowed down, her uncle said, "God bless you, and have prosperous life." After some casual talk about the next day's function, he promised to attend with his family and then quietly left. Sumi's eyes met her father's loving look, and both smiled.

Later, Mamu complimented, "Mohanbhai! You have done well. Believe me, it is easier to bless them than blame them. As the wise men say, 'A great man is he who does not sacrifice his child's heart to satisfy his ego.'"

The next morning, Sumi was awakened by the enchanting echo of the bells. She felt calm waves around her, and she was a lotus...She listened to the language of her soul as the shore listened to the murmur of the waves. They were saying, "All is well. All is well."

The commotion in the house was louder than usual due to two reasons: Kim and Nina. Sumi's parents had gone to their family jeweler to purchase gifts for Sumi and her new family. So the younger clan was in charge of the preparations.

The priest had given instructions on how to erect a puja mandap. It was built with banana leaves and decorated with many strings of torans. The torans were made with yellow marigolds and mango leaves tied with colorful threads. The torans were tied on the front door also as a part of the traditional welcome on the occasion of festivals and weddings.

Raju's parents, Mr. and Mrs. Mody, were welcomed honorably. About fifty relatives and friends were invited for the celebration. The bride and groom were seated in the center, following the priest's direction for homage. The puja was performed in reverence to the Lord Vishnu, the embodiment of truth.

The beautiful bride and charming groom were surrounded by their loved ones, dressed in a rainbow of colors. Under the cozy canopy, the sandalwood incense, the gentle bells, and happy laugh, Sumi was melted into the melodious evening.

The secret stolen stares were interlacing a love bridge between the two longing hearts.

The prayer concluded with an aarti, which consisted of Sumi and Raju circling a small firelit lamp in the vicinity of an image of the Lord. The guests were treated with a feast, prasad.

> The sad clouds had sailed away.
> The last rays of the setting sun
> hugged the newlyweds;
> a sweet welcome and farewell.

Early the next morning, Sumi and her new family planned to start their journey at crack of dawn. Raju greeted everyone, hugged Shan, and said, "Brother, see you in Vadodara next week." His family had planned a reception for the newlyweds on the following Sunday in Vadodara, and they all were expected to attend, including Mamu's family.

Sumi did pranam to her parents and completely broke down when she said good-bye to her brother.

Januma could not conceal her tears anymore. Sona had to come to her rescue. Sumi's father put his arm on Shan's shoulder to calm him. Sumi's sobbing continued on Raju's shoulder in the car until Ajay made her laugh.

Her New World

What a difference one generation to the next had made! Sumi's wedding was so different than her mother's. Januma was led into the marriage like a mute ignorant creature. And today, the daughter selected her husband and compelled the father to agree with her choice.

When they arrived at their home in Vadodara, Nina's parents were waiting to welcome them. Sumi entered her new home under sprinkles of kumkum and flowers. The auspicious, warm welcome filled her heart with gratitude.

As a married woman, she would wear a sari or similar traditional clothing; a mangalsutra, a gold necklace with black beads; and a bindi on her forehead, which is considered an essential symbol for a married woman. The area between the eyebrows is said to be the sixth chakra, the seat of "concealed wisdom." The bindi is said to retain energy and strengthen concentration. It also represents the third eye. The red color represents honor, love, and prosperity.

In modern times, the bindi is accepted as a fashion choice, which is not restricted to one religion or region. Sumi could choose the time and color of her bindi without upsetting the elderly relatives.

Before Raju's uncle and aunt went home, they invited the bride, groom, and family for dinner at their house. Papa Sam accepted his younger brother's invitation gladly.

At their uncle's house, Ajay seemed in a big hurry, and so was Nina. He asked several times, "When can we eat, Chachi?" So their aunt had to rush and serve them quickly. They finished eating and ran out of the house before the others were even half-finished.

Raju's uncle laughed and commented, "These crazy kids, always rushing to be somewhere and nowhere." To Sumi and Raju, their mysterious exit seemed quite comical.

The Modys returned home after a very pleasant evening. Raju went to his room. Sumi was about to follow him when she heard, "Dear Sumi! Please come here." Raju's mother was standing by the guest room.

"Yes, Mother," and she went to her.

Raju's mom led Sumi into the room and asked her to sit on the bed. She kindly said, "Sumi, I hope you are comfortable in your new home. I know you must be missing your mom and family. We are here for you and wholeheartedly welcome you...I am so glad that you came into my Raju's life. Because a woman symbolizes the future, you hold in your hand the soil of the past and the seeds of the future."

Sumi emotionally bowed her head and said, "Mother, bless me so I can bring more joy into this family. As my mom says, 'Families where the elders are respected by the younger generation, love and joy flow together—the good fortune follows.'"

"Yes, it is so true. I have heard about your mother from your uncle, and I admire her wisdom. So to welcome you, I have some special gifts for you." She handed three boxes to Sumi and said, "I am glad to present you with this heirloom jewelry. One set is diamonds, and one is made of real pearls. This third one is made of gold and platinum. It was given to me by my mom-in-law the day I came to this house as a bride. I have ordered some new designs for you, which should be ready soon. And here are a few saris and dresses. And, dear, you may call me Ammi, if you wish."

"Ammi! I like that." Sumi was overwhelmed with the shower of riches. She respectfully said, "I appreciate these gifts from the bottom of my heart, but this is more than enough. You know that I am a simple girl."

Her mother-in-law laughed and said, "I remember Ajay telling me the line about you in your college: 'Grace in simplicity and simplicity in grace.' Let me spoil my first daughter—a little?" Sumi giggled and agreed.

"Okay, we had a long day. It is time for you to get ready for the night, and Kantu will help you.

Now I leave you two alone. Nina should be here any minute." She had already instructed her trusted maid Kantu on how to help Sumi prepare for her first night with her husband.

After a sandalwood oil massage, Sumi bathed in fragrant rosewater. She put on a sky-blue silk nightdress under a matching satin nightgown trimmed with the finest embroidered lace and intricate motif. Kantu adorned Sumi's loosely braided hair with buds of mogra that matched her pearl earrings. Nina came and gave some final touches. She took the bashful bride to Raju's room and bid her good night.

Sumi opened the door and noticed her beloved standing near the swing in the moonlit veranda. The room was partially bright with candles. The gentle music and the fragrance of gardenia filled her heart with romantic excitement. She stepped into his room—her dreamed and desired world. The tinkle of her anklets attracted Raju's attention. He turned around, smiled, and came to greet her.

"Welcome to my world," Raju said. He held her velvety hand, and they softly glided toward the veranda. As soon as he saw Sumi in the silvery moonlight, he was mesmerized by her beauty. Their eyes did not see anything else, but they continued looking at each other as they stood there in a sweet embrace.

Sumi looked up and musingly said, "Wow! Finally, we are here! Remember, I had no hope that I would return to this home. Destiny has been kind to us."

"Yes. But let me thank my destiny!" Eagerly holding her hand, Raju took her to the swing and sat down. He looked mischievously at smiling Sumi. He spread his inviting arms and said, "Come to me, my sweet Suman, my flower."

Sumi hesitated and then shyly sat in the cradle of his arms. As his fingers explored her face delicately, her heart tickled with a fountain of delight. Her eyes closed, and she became submerged in deep inner joy.

"Tell me, what are you thinking, my love?" Raju whispered.

Sumi opened her eyes, full of emotions. She gently lifted her face and gave a sweet soft kiss to the awaiting lips. Then dreamily, she said, "I hear a melody rising from my heart. It hums like...I must have done something good in my life."

> *The cordial colors smile in the space.*
> *The hope star shines through the*
> *moonlight lace.*
> *Holy hue humbles and hugs me in verse;*
> *have I done some good to due deserved!*

She effortlessly slid by his side and sat encircled in Raju's arms. Raju said, "Darling! I am impressed with your spontaneous composition. Your romantic verse inspires me to create a painting that captures this night. Maybe soon I will do that, but right now I have a surprise for you. Let's go in."

Once inside the bedroom, she asked, "What is it?"

"You will have to find it."

Sumi thought, *I hope it is not jewelry.* She turned on the light and was pleasantly surprised to see the stylishly decorated room, especially the bed. The strings of flowers were tied to a focal point over the canopy, which covered the bed. The satin bedcovers had heart-shaped garlands and red rose petals sprinkled all around.

Sumi laughed and said, "So now we know why Ajay and Nina were in such a hurry!"

"Yes, I also did not know where those crazy kids were running to."

Raju pulled Sumi playfully in front of an easel and said, "Look, here is a portrait of my pretty girlfriend. If you are curious enough, you may remove the cover."

"Oh, no, why would I want to see her tonight?" Sumi playfully said, and she tried to walk away. But Raju did not let her go. So she complied. "Okay, if you insist."

Sumi removed the cover and happily teased, "Oh! You said your 'pretty girlfriend.' This one is just an average-looking girl."

"Not to me! I thought she looked exceptionally pretty that day." Raju had framed his memory of his meeting with Sumi at the Mumbai Railway Station more than a year ago. In the painting, Sumi, with braided hair and dressed in a simple shirt with pants, was shown seriously engaged in a conversation with her man on the train.

Sumi gently turned to him, looked up with her moist eyes, and said, "O My Raju! This is amazing. This is really a pleasant surprise. I do count my blessings that you saw this girl worthy of you."

She hugged him tightly and then wrapped her arms around his neck and whispered, "I love you." Raju lifted her up and held her close to his excitedly beating heart. His lips conveyed the message, "I love you too."

He brought her near the bed and tenderly put her down on the bed. The vibrations of a romantic song in a raga, Sohini, tantalized their beings…Raju sat next to her and murmured in her ear, "Sohini is a lovely form. Tall, virgin, charming, her eyes like lotuses, ears clustered with celestial flowers. She holds a lute, and her songs are amorous. You are my Sohini."

He pulled a string to open the flower-filled net overhead, and Sumi shivered with delight as the falling petals covered them. They embraced until their hearts melted.

The night had begun. Life had begun.

He wants to play with her silky soft lace.
He whispers to move the veil from her face.
The petals of their lips open and close;
the pearls on her chest play hide-and-seek.
O my love! I clearly see,
God has made you just for me!

Footprints on the Grass

The serene sound of the prayer song streamed in on a ray of morning sun to awaken Sumi. She was adrift in a reverie of joy, relived during the few hours of deep sleep. She was in a different world…A rising question, "Where am I?" was followed by a content smile as she looked at her peacefully sleeping husband. And she felt waves of luring affection all over again.

She got up quickly to get ready like a dutiful daughter-in-law. Right after the bath, she resumed her usual routine of sitting in quiet for a few moments.

Dressed in a beautiful sari and matching jewelry, she was ready to face the new family. She noiselessly came near Raju and stared at his handsome face. As she turned to go away, she saw that the edge of her sari was caught in his fist. He opened his sleepy eyes. Sumi sat down next to him and planted a kiss on his forehead. He held her close and kissed her cheeks while they became gently red like the first ray of dawn. Sumi hurriedly went out of the room before it could become a longer interlude.

Her father-in-law was reading the newspaper, and her mom-in-law was getting the tea and breakfast ready.

It was obvious that they both were enjoying the bhajan playing on the radio. Sumi entered the kitchen and said, "Pranam, Ammi."

"Bless you, dear. Did you sleep well? If anything needs to be changed in your room, let me know." She observed closely and seemed satisfied to see the pleasant expressions on Sumi's face.

Soon after her, Raju came out of his room and said, "Good morning, everyone. First of all, a good cup of tea, right, Ma?"

"Sure." His mother looked at him and then at his father, and they both exchanged a secret grin. Sumi noticed that exchange between his parents. So she looked at Raju. There was a round dot of kumkum on his shirt sleeve.

She was mortified. *Oh! No! How embarrassing,* she thought.

Sumi signaled him, but before he could realize it, they heard Ajay's voice. "See, I can get up early too… Oh! Bhai, since when did you start wearing a bindi on your sleeve?" He would not pass up a chance to tease his brother. Perplexed, Raju quickly rolled up his sleeves.

They all gathered on the porch. With cups of tea in hand, the ideas about the reception poured in. The venue was decided as the Paradise Resort. It was a new attraction designed for wealthy families to have parties and mini vacations. This kind of resort had been established recently near only a few big cities, and Sumi had not seen one so far. She had no clue how big the event was going to be until she saw the bigwig names on the guest list.

Her father-in-law addressed her, saying, "Beta, Sumi! We have invited most of your relatives. Now you may want to extend the invitations to your friends and your former professors here at the university!"

"Thank you, Father. I will make a list and show you," Sumi said.

In the afternoon when Sumi showed him the list of the people she wanted to invite, her father-in-law readily consented. Then he showed her the invitation card, designed by Raju. "Please give me your opinion and whether any changes are needed," he said. Sumi was so touched by this simple gesture. She loved the design and suggested keeping her name "Sumi," instead of "Suman" on the invitation cards.

When she returned the card to her father-in-law, he looked at it and smiled from ear to ear. He turned to his wife and said, "Listen, what your daughter has added to the line. 'No gifts please. Your presence is the precious present for the bride and groom.'"

The week flew by like the clouds with the wind. On the night before the reception, the music and mehndi evening was organized. A professional henna artist started to draw with henna paste from a cone-shaped tube with a tiny hole. Sumi's palms were designed with the intricate geometric patterns, with the hidden letter *R* for her beloved, Raju. The use of mehndi and turmeric is intended to be a symbolic representation of the outer and the inner sun. Vedic customs are centered on the idea of "awakening the inner light." Traditional Indian designs are representations of the sun on the palm.

After they picked up Anu and Priya from the railway station, the boys also joined the party and demanded some mehndi designs on their hands. Raju was challenged to find the letter *R* in Sumi's palm. While Anu and Priya teased Raju, Sumi stayed at his side. The merriment continued past midnight.

On the day of the reception, Sumi's family came around noontime. She could see that her father was feeling awkward among the sophisticated high-class people even though they were going out of their way to make him feel comfortable. Mamu had been able to convince Sumi's father to come along with the assurance that they would return home the same night.

Right after lunch, the ladies started getting ready with the help of the beauticians from the salon. Then Sumi, dressed in her custom-made lehenga, looked beautiful. A long pleated skirt made of heavy silk, looked elegant with gold-thread embroidery and gemstone appliqué and border work. Made with net and velvet material, the long red choli showed off her lovely figure. An exquisite dupatta, a sign of modesty and grace, flowed down the front and back from her shoulder.

Her bangles and earrings
her necklace and rings;
her glowing beauty reflected her feelings.
She had learned the eternal secret
of giving and receiving the boundaryless
love.

Since the Mody family was very particular about arriving on time at the Paradise Resort, Sumi and Raju had a few minutes to enjoy the tamed nature. The guests started trickling in, and then there was a commotion…"Member of Parliament, Mr. Mehta, has arrived."

Sumi grabbed Raju's arm and whispered, "Please, just stay close to me." Raju was confused but followed her cue. Mr. Mody greeted the guests and brought them to the bride and groom.

As soon as Mr. Mehta looked at Sumi, he exclaimed, "Oh! Suman, if I am not mistaken."

"Yes, sir. Namaste," she replied. Then he turned to talk with Raju.

Mrs. Mehta deliberately paused in front of Sumi and spoke under her breath. "Congratulations…I knew it. You wanted to do something like this, so you nixed my son," she said. The last words fell on Raju's ears, which he couldn't believe. The woman flashed a fake smile at both of them and walked away. Sumi was shaken inside. The bitter woman left Sumi distressed and momentarily overshadowed her cheery mood. Luckily, the Mehtas left shortly after that rude remark.

The evening was filled with hugs, laughs, and music. Sumi and Januma were very emotional at times. Her father was somber among so many strangers. Shan and Sona promised to come back for a visit very soon. When they left, Sumi smiled and waved good-bye, standing along with her new family. "What! No more tears?" Raju teased.

That night, Sumi explained to Raju why Mrs. Mehta was angry at her and then forgot about the incident. They had to start preparations for Sumi's entry visa to the USA. Everything had to be ready before January. The short time they had with the family was precious. They avoided mentioning their departure as much as possible because it made his mother sad.

It had been a week since the reception day. Sumi prepared the afternoon tea and brought it into the living room. Her father-in-law was opening the mail. He seemed very upset looking at one letter.

"I can't believe this! Raju, you remember that social project I was trying to get approval for? It has been rejected by Mr. Mehta, who had earlier praised the idea immensely," he said.

Raju was quiet for a while, and then he looked at Sumi. She was panicked to see her father-in-law angry. She hesitantly spoke, "Father! Maybe, I could be the reason for it…It was my second semester here in Vadodara. A few months prior, the Mehta family had seen me at my cousin's wedding. They are of our caste and are respected as a high-class family. They had asked my parents' permission to visit me in Vadodara while they were in town. When they came to meet me at the hostel, they were very sure that I would not even remotely think of refusing their son's proposal. But Mrs. Mehta and her son seemed rude and crude individuals to me. And when he took out a cigarette to smoke, I ran the other direction as fast as I could."

"Oh! Bhabhi! You have sinned by rejecting the mighty Mehtas," Ajay teased.

They all laughed. "The way Mrs. Mehta showed her anger toward Sumi at the reception proved what kind of people they are," Raju said.

"Well, whatever the reason may be, this is unfair, and I will have to pursue the matter for the greater good. But you don't worry about it, dear," her father-in-law said. That was Sumi's first experience with her father-in-law's anger. She admired his ascendancy of wisdom and grace over his anger.

Every hour of the day, Sumi was learning about her new family members. She felt that her words and actions were the building blocks for their future relationships. In this spring of her life, what she planted would manifest multifold. She wanted to nurture such a seed, which could grow into a gorgeous tree to give everyone the peaceful shade.

It was a lovely evening. The family was enjoying a delicious dessert on the patio. "Ammi! Do we know how many girlfriends Ajay has?" Sumi asked her mother-in-law.

"Not sure, because I have met only one or two," she replied.

"Yes, which is the right count. Now, Bhabhi! Don't mock me. Okay, tell me, how do you know which person is right for me?" Ajay inserted.

"The person to whom you are instantly attracted to," Raju said, and he shot a lively look toward Sumi.

"A girl who likes your parents," his mother laughingly said.

"The one who brings out the best in you," Sumi thoughtfully said.

Ajay turned to his father and said, "Papa, you tell me, who has the right idea?"

"They all are right, and furthermore, the one who brings out the best in you would be the best kind of life partner—in my opinion," he said.

"I see...you are on Sumi's side," his mother exclaimed. It was obvious that Sumi had earned the family members' love and respect in a short time.

Raju and Sumi did not want to go on a honeymoon, which would cut their time with the family. But they did have to go to Mumbai for her visa to the USA. That was their first time alone together, and they cherished it. At that time, they spent one day with her cousin Risa in Mumbai, who was her guide in that bustling city.

That year, the Diwali was celebrated in November. The Hindu calendar depends on the movement of the sun and moon. The festival of light celebrates the victory of good over evil, light over darkness, and knowledge over ignorance; although, the actual legends that go with the festival are different in different parts of India. In northern India and elsewhere, Diwali celebrates Rama's return from fourteen years of exile to Ayodhya after the defeat of Ravana and his subsequent coronation as king. In Gujarat, the festival honors Lakshmi, the goddess of wealth, and so on.

Diwali time brought the excitement and joy. The world around them was humming with new energy. Sumi's one-week visit with her parents, Shan and Sona, and the extended family satiated her heart. Raju also joined them since it was their last possible visit before they would leave for the USA.

Januma had a hard time letting go of her daughter. She was tormented by two thoughts. One thought was telling her to be happy for Sumi's bright future with a good life partner. On the other hand, her fretful heart could not be convinced to accept the fact that her only daughter would be living in a faraway country. Januma had no idea about the way of life in America. The fear of the unknown was greater than the real thing.

Well, she buried her head down in her grief and, day by day, tried to untie her knotted emotions.

Sumi barely had time to identify with the agony of her mother's heart. Her world was filled with curious wonders of the magic land.

> The wedding spell had passed,
> leaving footprints on her heart.
> They softly pressed the joy
> to her bosom day and night.

Promises to Keep

I am a beautiful pearl...
When I cry, the hills laugh;
When I humble myself, the flowers rejoice;
When I bow, all things are elated...
I am the sigh of the sea;
The laughter of the field;
The tears of heaven...

—Kahlil Gibran (*Song of the Rain*)

Sumi was reading Kahlil Gibran's poem. A teardrop rolled down from the corner of her eye. Raju held that precious pearl on the tip of his finger and said, "I suppose this pearl is a testimony of the joy I see on your face!"

Sumi responded happily. "Yes. Listen to this lovely poem." And she recited the poem to him. Raju stroked her hair, and the raga Malhaar was evoked inside...She finished reading, but the rain outside kept on singing. Sumi put her hand in his hand, and without a word, they both walked into the small patio amidst the pouring rain. The raindrops embraced them with a cool breeze, and their racing hearts kept them warm. They melted in the rain with sighs of deep affection, laughter, and fervent passion…And that's how the evening turned into the night, and days turned into months in their new home in California. The whisper in the air lyrically said, "How beautiful life is, my beloved. It is like the poet's heart filled with light and tenderness."

They had been in America for about two months. Raju and Sumi had rented a one-bedroom apartment on the university campus. Leaving India was hard, but the gray cloud of exodus was blown away quickly by the bright light of the promised land. Raju started his work soon after their arrival in California, and Sumi was left to learn about her new life on her own. She enjoyed every adventure and laughed about her blunders and bloopers.

The secondhand car and their basic needs were eating away at his postdoctoral fellowship money. Sumi's two prized possessions were a passion flower vine and a plant of queen's rose—both inherited from the previous owner of that apartment. She started looking for a job within the limitations of her visa restriction. It did not seem likely for her to find a job suitable to her qualifications, so she decided to take any job she could find on campus.

Sumi finally landed a job as a lab assistant. She was forced to forget about the 'Doctor Suman' title for a while. Since childhood, she had been taught the philosophy of their holy book, the Bhagavad Gita. Her mind was telling her that the time had come for her to put her knowledge into practice. One shloaka was pulsating in her consciousness…

कर्मणयेवाधिकिारस्ते मा फलेषु कदाचन।
मा कर्मफलहेतुर्भूर्मा ते सइग्गोऽस्त्वकर्मणि

"Karmanye vadhikaraste, ma phaleshou kada chana." You have the right to perform your actions, but you are not entitled to the fruits of the actions.

"Ma karma phala hetur bhurmatey sangostva akarmani." Do not let the fruit be the purpose of your actions, and therefore, you won't be attached to not doing your duty.

Sumi interpreted this wisdom in her mind as no work is lower or higher. She would perform every task with the best of her abilities.

On the first day of work, she felt like a lost deer in the forest. Her English differed from the American English. Talking with some individuals, she wondered, "Are we communicating in the same language?" Sumi was embarrassed and also amused a little to see the dubious look on some faces, which announced, "I will not understand anything that comes out of this brown person's mouth."

Some kindhearted professionals guided her in the lab work. The routine, simple, and common lab work was new to her. She felt that any simpleminded person would do a better job than she did. Those eight hours seemed very long.

She came out of the building and sat in the waiting car. She avoided looking at Raju. "How was your day?" he asked. Sumi's eyes flooded with tears—unexpectedly. Raju was stunned to see her cry and could not say anything for some time. He turned off the car and held her. After a few minutes, Sumi composed herself and asked Raju to drive the car.

Back at their apartment, Sumi changed her clothes, freshened up, and came out. Raju was waiting for her with a glass of orange juice. "Come and sit here. We will cook later. Now tell me what happened!" he said.

Sumi spoke in her weepy voice, "Nothing specific. The whole day's humiliation broke the limit when my senior technician handed me the broom at the end of the day to clean up my work area. Back home in my lab, I was a scholar. The different surrounding was hard to take. These unexpected tears must be from my bruised, rebellious ego," She tried to smile.

"I know that this job is below your dignity. I am not saying that you should continue, but in this country, I see that people take any job to survive and use it as a stepping stone to reach their goal," Raju kindly said.

"I understand. I also know that I will learn many things. But still, this is so degrading," Sumi said. She sounded discouraged.

"Okay! It is simple. You should not continue this job. I do not want to see you unhappy." There was a faint shadow of disappointment in his voice.

Sumi remained quiet, lost in her thoughts.

"I am starved. Let's go out for a pizza," Raju said.

The next morning, Raju heard some noise in the kitchen. He was surprised to see Sumi ready in her work clothes. She was filling up two lunch boxes. "Are you sure you want to go to work?" Raju asked.

"Yes, I am mentally ready. I think I used up all my tears yesterday."

Raju laughed and said, "I'm sure…they will be freshly manufactured again soon."

On the way to work, Raju said, "I forgot to tell you my associate, Anil, has invited us for dinner this Saturday. His wife, Rashi, works in the admission office. Should I say yes?"

"Yes, that would be nice," Sumi gladly said.

As the week passed, Sumi felt better about her job.

The cool Saturday evening breeze was swaying the lush trees, putting Sumi in a nostalgic mood. She felt that she was walking on the farm surrounded by the mango trees, with her friend Anu.

> A wisp of wind flew her thousands of miles.
> She saw a little girl on a branch of a tree.
> She ate stolen sour mango and made funny face.
> She was proud of her crime and flaunted a smile.

She delayed looking up, as if she did not want to replace the mango trees with the oak trees of California.

Anil and Rashi lived in walking distance from Raju and Sumi's apartment. It turned out to be a very pleasant evening for all of them. Sumi was intrigued. Rashi was from a Hindu family and married to a white American Catholic.

"I expected a brown face behind this Indian name 'Anil.' How come?" Sumi asked.

"Oh! It is funny," Rashi explained. "His given name was Nil, but he changed it to Anil to impress me when we met in a yoga class. He also became vegetarian. That's why his mother is quite annoyed with us." Rashi's jolly good laugh was contagious. Sumi felt that she had found a friend in this foreign land. They both planned to do some "girl" things together.

Sumi eased into her work slowly and found some friends, so she did not have to eat lunch alone. On the weekends, she regularly wrote letters to both sides of the familiy. The main link of communication with their loved ones back home was through letters. It made her day when she would receive the blue aerogram from India. In the early 1970s, phone calls were expensive and needed preplanning on the both sides due to the eleven-hour time difference and connection problems.

Raju was spending a lot more time in the lab, so Sumi would to go out with Rashi a couple of times a week. Sumi used to talk about her family often, but Rashi's response was very impassive, especially when Sumi talked about her mother. Sumi noticed that Rashi had a deep, suppressed anger that sporadically flared.

One day, with an annoyed expression, Rashi said, "My in-laws are coming to visit us—for ten days. They are coming next Thursday."

"Hey, that's nice...isn't it?" Sumi good-naturedly said.

"I can't stand my mother-in-law!" Rashi said.

Sumi was shocked to hear that. *How can you feel that way about the mother whose son you claim to love!* she thought. Sumi refrained from making any comment.

It was Anil's birthday on Saturday, and Rashi had invited many people. Sumi went to help in the afternoon. She met Rashi's father-in-law and Anil outside on the patio. Her mother-in-law, Marie, was working hard in the kitchen. Rashi looked busy but did not seem to accomplish much. The tension between them was so thick she could not have cut it with a knife. Sumi's presence made things easier, and the preparations were completed.

In the evening, on the way to the party, Sumi told Raju, "I don't know what the problem is! Rashi's mother-in-law seemed like a nice lady. So many times, Rashi whispered and whined in my ear about her while I was there this afternoon. Beware. Sparks could fly."

Raju took it as a joke until he entered their domain and felt the vibes. There were only a few guests. Rashi seemed perturbed by two calls she had received. One was from Anil's sister, who had changed her plans at the last minute and had decided to hang out with her friends. The second call troubled her more because two of her cousins' families were on their way, a two-hour drive, to their house; but their car had broken down, and they had to cancel.

They all tried to be upbeat, but still the birthday party was celebrated in a somber mood.

It was a lazy Sunday morning, the day after Anil's birthday party. Sumi had prepared an ample pot of chai tea with fresh ginger and cardamom, rich with more milk than water. At that time, they were surprised to hear a knock at the door. "So early in the morning! Who that could be?" Raju wondered as he opened the door. Anil's father was at the door.

"Oh! Good morning, sir! What a pleasant surprise," Raju said.

"Oh! I shouldn't have disturbed you," the nervous father said. He looked at Sumi and seemed to find his courage. "Do you mind if I talk to you for a few minutes?"

"Namaste. Please come in," Sumi greeted him. They kindly led him inside and handed him a cup of tea.

"I don't know what to say...Rashi did not sleep last night, and neither did we. I suppose you are her friend, so I came to talk to you."

"Yes, please."

Sumi and Raju were aware of the tension in that family so did not bother him with questions. "After the guests had left, we were just casually talking about the leftover food, etcetera. We don't even remember what my wife Marie said, but Rashi's face turned red. She went and locked herself in her bedroom, leaving everything as it was.

"Marie and I were puzzled and embarrassed by that reaction. Anil was confused also. After several requests, she let Anil in their bedroom, and we heard arguments afterward. It was close to midnight. Rashi came out of her room and exited from the front door in a rage. Anil went after her and, holding her wrist, firmly pulled her back into the house. For the rest of the night, I put a chair across the door and sat there…

"Marie and I have never felt so unwanted anywhere and never imagined that we would feel out of place in our child's home."

Raju kindly put his hand on his shoulder. "How sad," Sumi uttered. The sorrow of a father's voice touched the core of her heart. "What can I do? Should I go and talk to her sometime today?"

"Anil has not been able to convince her to come out of her bedroom this morning. Please, can you try—soon?" he ruefully said.

Sumi assured him that she would come in a few minutes. As soon as Sumi arrived, Anil and his parents seemed relieved. Their ashen faces showed some normal brightness.

Sumi entered Rashi's bedroom and pulled a chair near her bed. Rashi opened her puffy eyes and was astonished to see Sumi there.

"Hey, girlfriend! Good morning. Time to wake up…" Sumi said. Rashi turned her head away to hide the tears. Sumi held her hand and said, "Come on, Rashi! Tell me, what is bothering you?"

"Nobody likes me. They all are on one side, and I am alone. Marie wants to be near her son. That is why she is so sweet and all that with me. Why can't she be like my mother, who never pretends to care for me?" Rashi grumbled.

Sumi realized that some old, brewing emotions had been triggered, and now she was finding faulty reasons, boosted by her ego, to justify her behavior. "You may be right, but now is the time to go out and have a cup of tea. Come, get up."

Rashi and Sumi came out of the bedroom, and Anil greeted them. They sat at the table while Marie brought them tea and some snacks. It seemed as though each one was reluctant to speak first. Sumi talked about the weather. Sumi was thinking, *How can Rashi do this? No apology, no nothing!*

Finally, when Marie started to clear the table, Rashi got up and said, "I will do it."

Sumi was embarrassed for her friend's behavior, but that was not the proper time to say anything. She looked at poor Anil, who was caught between two relations closest to his heart. "I will see you all soon," Sumi meaningfully said and went home.

Anil called later and talked to Sumi, "At times, Rashi is so loving and gentle, while at other times— like yesterday—horrible. I do not see any love in her eyes. It is as if I do not know her. Anyway, I will take her out in the evening. My parents will be home. I will appreciate it if…"

"Don't worry. Raju and I will go and keep them company."

Sumi went to Anil's home in the evening. "Raju will join us later. I know that we do not know each other well, but you remind me of my parents," she said.

"I feel that I can talk to you. From the beginning, Rashi ignored our importance in Anil's life. For her, we are a nuisance," Marie said.

"She shows us no appreciation for anything we have done. The good life they have been living due to Anil's good education at a top university or this house we helped them to purchase…never a thank you from her. The nicer we get, more resentful and rude she becomes," Anil's father said.

"First, we thought that Anil is responsible for allowing her to treat us like this. But now we can see that her twisted mind is closed tight behind a volatile ego. She seems unreasonable and unreachable," Marie said bitterly.

"I see you both are very disappointed. As parents, you both have so much love to give, but a heart has to be open to receive it. In this case, before it consumes your happiness, pray for her. That will keep you in a serene space and keep a peaceful link with your son. Hopefully, Rashi will recognize her pain and find the help to heal. We hope that she chooses to allow the love and joy to flow into this relationship.

"She is a nice person underneath. Please give them some time. I humbly suggest that you do not allow any interruption in the link that ties you to your son."

Raju came, and they talked more over the leftover food. A simple evening turned into a memorable one. Anil's parents felt better, especially the loving mother, who was crushed under the guilt of hurting Rashi's feelings. Sumi helped Marie to realize that some people have their own demons to deal with, and they seek vulnerable targets to release their anger. After they went home, Raju turned on the classical Sufi music. They both cuddled on the sofa and were submerged in the soulful music.

The next day, Anil told them that his parents were leaving in the afternoon. Rashi asked them halfheartedly to stay, but they would not.

The following Saturday, Sumi and Rashi took a long walk in the park and then sat down under a grand oak tree. Rashi again showed dislike toward her in-laws in their casual conversation.

"Tell me, why are you so resentful toward Anil's parents?" Sumi asked.

The one-sided outlook window opened, and words poured out, colored with her perception. "They never liked me," Rashi said.

"You have entered into their small world, so you have to do things so they like you. Isn't this a normal procedure?" Sumi's logical mind asked a question that Rashi ignored.

"Marie says things to taunt me. For example, that night, the things she said about the leftover food, 'Nice, you will have some good food to eat for a few days,' I know she implied that I do not cook good food for her son. When she says, 'I will help to clean up,' it means I am lazy. And Anil does not hear that because she is *his* mother."

The internal irritation was burning her. The perception was so irrational that it made Sumi smile. She remembered Marie had said, "I open my mouth, and Rashi gets offended!"

The more they talked, the more Rashi felt the dark layers inside her unfolding. She was shocked to see that her suppressed anger was spreading sad ashes on her present moments. Some of the bitterness was totally unrelated to her current relations.

Sumi said, "The thing is, his mother is now your mother too. You have to resolve this knotted attitude, these conflicts that make you miserable. Personally,

I believe that they are your husband's parents and deserve respect from both of you.

"I am your friend, and I gently request you to open your heart and let the love flow in. In the game of blame and judgment, introspection is the only way out. You will see that the controversies are arising from your mind. We do not have control upon what people say, but we have control on how we interpret... And one more thing, the attitude of 'they should take care of me' results in disappointment on your side and resentment on their side."

They talked in depth about the effects of her behavior and Anil's position. Rashi listened silently and showed faint willingness to think differently. She did not see many options if she wanted to keep her marriage intact.

Sumi and Rashi's meeting turned out to be a spiritual session. "I think I am a proactive person in the area of peace of my mind. It is my valuable asset, and I do not want to lose it," Sumi said.

"How do you keep your peace safe?" Rashi asked.

"I think if you keep the anger suppressed within and show off superficial courtesy, the lava inside you will blow up at any moment by an unforeseen trigger. So we have to work inside out, and keep the peace in the safe box of our hearts. And I do that with three steps: observe, accept, and let go. One has to observe, with awareness, so no one can fool you. Accept, with gratitude, because everything around us is a God-given gift. And learn to let go, because in life, good or bad, everything will pass—no matter how hard you try to hold on!" Sumi expressed the essence of her wisdom candidly.

They both sat in silence, staring at the blooming nature, but not seeing. Sumi had to peek inside her soul and truthfully observe that how closely she had been able to follow this wisdom. Rashi had to analyze whether Sumi's wisdom made any sense to her or not!

"I will have to mull over this different way of thinking. But I admit this much. After many days, today I feel free of that dull, aching pinch in my heart. I have to find inner courage to choose a path of love. Otherwise, I will be destroyed in the path of aversion," Rashi said.

Affliction bangs its head in the dark,
at the barriers built of yours and mine.
There, the fragile feelings are brashly
broken.
The graceful waves are rashly trodden.
Affection travels quite free in elation,
Go take a chance to revel in relations.
Petals of lotus link smile to smile,
in wide-open space from eye to eye.

"I have read somewhere, 'Emotion is energy in motion, and if you do not let it flow, it becomes too heavy and crushes your spirit.' You will see that the simple and uncomplicated relations with your in-laws will bring you so much peace and joy. If I speak honestly, please do not drag the pain from your other relations into this one... You know what I mean?" Sumi said.

Rashi thought about her mother and her siblings and said, "I see myself clearly now. Wow! What have I been doing to Anil's loving parents?" Sumi felt satisfied, closing the conversation. After a few weeks, she felt really good when Anil and Rashi came and talked about their "okay" visit with his parents.

That Friday, Raju came home and announced, "You have done great job helping Rashi, so in appreciation, Anil is taking us to the Los Angeles Philharmonic Orchestra. Music Director Zubin Mehta is conducting Johann Strauss's compositions this Saturday."

That was Sumi's first experience, and she deeply enjoyed the music. On the way home, she said, "I had a hard time controlling my tears when I heard "On the Beautiful Blue Danube." That composition touched my heart."

Soul-Searching

Lately, Sumi was not feeling well. Raju was totally submerged in his project. At times, Sumi resented the lonely evenings and weekends. But one day, she got some great news about her brother, Shan. He was selected for the youth exchange program and was coming to the USA within days. He was to come to her place first and then travel to different states for three weeks. He would stay with them for a couple of days more at the end of his journey before his return to India.

She was delighted to welcome her dear brother, her longest and strongest relation. Shan's arrival coincided with Rakhi Day. Sumi invited many Indian and non-Indian friends for the festivity.

Sumi explained what she and some of her Indian friends were doing. "In India, this Rakhi festival is celebrated for brothers and sisters to express their deep emotional ties. On this special day, the sister ties a rakhi, a simple cotton or silk thread, to the wrist of her brother and puts a tilaka on his forehead, with a prayer for his well-being. In return, her brother makes a promise to take care of his sister. Usually, the brother gives gift to the sister to mark the occasion. The sentiment that surrounds the festival is unsurpassed. Amidst the merriment, the rituals are also intertwined with deep feelings of sacred loyalty and great devotion."

When Sumi tied a rakhi on Shan's right wrist, the tears of joy covered her cheeks. She recited her poem.

> Years have gone by since our childhood departed.
> Always wish you well from the bottom of my heart.
> The gentle subtle feelings are wrapped in a string.
> This soft shiny silk prays all the joy to bring.

They offered a piece of sweet to each other. The guests were surprised to see Rashi tying a rakhi to Raju. Sumi smiled and said, "You can tie it to anyone if you have brotherly affection for that person."

When Shan and Sumi had a quiet time, they talked about the situation back home. Sumi knew that her mom was having a hard time coping without her daughter in India. Shan told her about one incident.

It was about four months after Sumi was gone. Sumi's friend Priya was visiting her parents' home. Priya heard a knock on the door around ten o'clock at night. Surprisingly, Januma was at the door. "She had said, 'Sorry, dear, for coming so late, but I had to see your face. I miss Sumi,' and she hugged Priya…"

Silent sorrow filled Sumi's heart, and it ached for her mother.

Raju and Sumi had planned a visit to Yosemite National Park, and it worked out perfectly when Shan was with them. Anil and Rashi also joined them, so five of them loaded into a car and proceeded on the pilgrimage. As the naturalist, John Muir said, "Yosemite National Park *is by far the grandest of all the special temples of Nature I was ever permitted to enter.*"

After about three hours of driving from the city of San Francisco, they entered the majestic, green, peaceful remoteness of the Mariposa Grove of Giant Sequoias.

The Yosemite National Park is best known for its waterfalls, but within its nearly 1,200 square miles, you can find deep valleys, grand meadows, ancient giant sequoias, a vast wilderness area, and the 2,425-foot Yosemite Falls, which ranks as the tallest in North America, flowing down into the scenic valley meadows. Two wild and scenic rivers, the Tuolumne and Merced Rivers, begin in the park and flow west to the Central Valley. The visitors take notice of the enormous granite mountains from the 8,842-foot Half Dome to the 13,114-foot Mt. Lyell, Yosemite's tallest peak.

After reading about the beautiful park, Shan sighed, "Oh! I wish Sona could have been here."

"O my poor dear brother is missing his sweetie pie. Well, next time…Shan! You told me there were two reasons why Sona could not come. One was the expense, but you did not tell me about the second reason. When we were rushing out this morning, you got a call from Sona. What was that about?" Sumi teased him.

"Well, I was waiting for a special moment for this announcement, but I cannot hold off any longer," Shan excitedly said. "Before I left India, we suspected that Sona was pregnant, and this morning, it was confirmed!" Cheers and hugs went on and on.

The happy campers arrived at their lodging destination and checked in. They explored as much as they could in the remaining daylight hours. Night brought a deep surrounding sound of the falling water. For Sumi, the feeling was too wonderful for words. She sat there, gently leaning on Raju's arm under the open sky. They just looked at the breathtaking scenic vistas and almost touched the dark night sky above.

The next morning, their exploration started way before the sun came up. The valley was lined with beautiful wildflowers surrounded by the green mountains layered with the picturesque western juniper, Jeffrey, and ponderosa pines. Hiking and bicycling were done to reach the midway point. The bus ride on the road to Glacier Point coiled through the forest and around lush meadows. The panoramic view from Glacier Point showed a tremendous sweep of the length of the valley in both directions. They looked down into a world of miniature people, cars, and buildings. The Merced River was like a tiny creek, and the roads, like a network of dark ribbons.

After that memorable trip to Yosemite, Shan left for three weeks. Sumi was happily looking forward to his return visit. She resumed her routine. But in about two weeks, she felt feverish and weak again. That week Raju was very busy working on his presentation. As on many other evenings, he had come home late. Sumi had prepared supper but had gone to bed early with a high fever and also with the fervent feelings of neglect. In the morning when she told Raju about her fever, he was concerned. He told her to go to the campus clinic, but helplessly disappeared under the load of his busy schedule. Sumi was irritated and decided to stay in bed.

"Sumi! How come you did not show up at my presentation?" Raju was disappointed when he returned home in the early afternoon. Sumi was sitting on the sofa, motionless. As soon as she tried to speak, she began to cough incessantly. Raju threw down his briefcase and ran to the kitchen to get a glass of water. His face drained when Raju realized how sick Sumi had been. His disappointment turned into guilt. He decided to take her to the main hospital, even though she did not have an appointment. Fortunately, a seasoned doctor was on duty, and he squeezed her in as a last patient. After the checkup and lab tests, they were told to go home and wait for his call.

The next day, Shan came back. He was worried to see his sister so sick. They were waiting for the call from the doctor's office. It was early evening, and the looming clouds were a dark omen in Sumi's mind. The four observing eyes reflected Sumi's mood.

The phone rang, and when she heard the doctor himself on the line, her heart sank. "Mrs. Mody! This is a rare case, but it is confirmed that you have tuberculosis," he said. Raju saw fright on her face and took the receiver from her. The doctor asked Raju to keep Sumi in isolation and bring her to the hospital early in the morning. The three were stunned. Only Sumi's coughing was breaking the silence. The sharp edge of grave possibilities was searing inside, breaking her courage to pieces.

"Sumi, the doctor was quite confident that you will be okay…He has instructed you to make a list of the people you have been in contact with during the last couple of weeks. They should all be notified and tested for TB," Raju said.

Sumi couldn't decide what was worse, getting this disease or everyone knowing about it! Immediately, she thought about her in-laws and her parents. She imagined, *When Shan goes back and tells my parents, how will they react? Oh! I hope…he does not have to say, "Sumi is no more."*

Before her tears became too visible, Sumi got up and said, "I will pack my bag," and she disappeared to her bedroom. Raju was confused about how to console her. She seemed so detached and distant. This last call had come as a sharp arrow, and those three hearts were bleeding profusely. Growing up in India, they had heard the word *TB* was connected with the word *death*.

Shan suggested Raju to play Sumi's favorite music while he went to bring her out of her room. Sumi came and sat in a chair, not next to anyone on the sofa. Her red eyes had a faraway look. She started general conversation, but eventually, they had to address the present situation. Sumi had to show Raju how she had arranged the kitchen. She handed a big package of gifts to Shan to take with him to India. Raju told Sumi not to worry because she would be back very soon from the hospital, but she was not listening.

"I am so thankful for your presence at this time," Sumi told Shan before she went to bed. Shan gave her a compassionate smile and lay down on a sleeping bag in the living room. Raju hugged Sumi in the privacy of their bedroom, but Sumi pulled away and handed him a pillow to go and sleep somewhere else. Raju went to the living room and stretched out on the sofa.

He had never felt so alone and helpless before. He wished that his parents or at least his brother, Ajay, could have been there. He was shaken thinking about a future without his Suman. He had almost forgotten his life before Sumi. He felt paralyzed, and tears rolled from his eyes, soaking his pillow.

The hospital staff was instructed to keep the patient Mrs. Sumi Mody under quarantine. As soon as she was settled in the room, Dr. Tate came in, wearing a mask and gown, followed by Raju and Shan wearing similar garb. Sumi felt terrible for getting this contagious disease and troubling so many people.

The doctor outlined the course of the treatment, and they all left her alone in her isolation. She was taken to the lab for more X-rays and tests. The ordeal was unbearable. When she was brought back to her room, the coughing started, and for the first time, she saw the bright red tinge in her sputum.

Her own thoughts were dragging her away from her life. Sumi thought, till last week, she did not even think that she would ever grow old. And today, she succumbed to the end of her life.

She lay in the bed and thought about her loved ones and her short journey with her beloved Raju.

Like a flower of His sigh, I will curl up and
die.
I wish you, o my love, you flourish and
survive.

She held her mother's soft silk scarf near her cheeks and feebly went to sleep in her mother's lap.

Sumi was uncomfortable and half-asleep. Her mind was running a mile a minute. So she decided to keep it occupied by making the list of her belongings. She first thought about Shan and Sona. She was glad that Shan had his own family, a loving wife, and a child on the way. Sumi smiled when she thought of Priya. The list of things started to roll. "I will give my banarasi silk sari to Priya and to Anu..." The list continued reasonably well. Sumi was surprised to think about the people whom she had forgotten since ages.

The final question flashed, which startled her. "What do I leave for my ma and papa?" Sumi started to cry like a little girl. The sobbing made her breathing difficult. She pulled herself on her feet, drank some water, and turned on the TV.

She calmed down and composed a letter in her mind.

Ma, if you had to make a choice,
to have me for some time or not at all.
What would you choose?

Hold My Hand

Your heart is restless,
and tears roll from the corners of the eyes.
Are they yours or mine?
I know sweetheart! You feel so low,
but are you ready to go?
Yes, I know, you are in great pain.
But I have great love for you.
Tell me, if I love you more, do you have less
pain?
Will it hurt less, if I love you more?

Sumi woke up with alarm. Raju was there holding her hand. "What happened? Where am I?" she questioned. She saw her meal on the side stand. The doctor was writing on the chart. She was jolted forward into the present when she saw the masks and gowns on everyone.

"Dear, you were asleep for a while. Dr. Tate wants to brief us about your condition," Raju said.

"Sumi, your disease is in its second stage. You will be getting an injection every day for the next five days. You will be given two kinds of pills. You will be in quarantine for at least ten days. You are young, and the bug has been caught in its early stages. The prognosis is good," Dr. Tate said.

The news brought some relief. Raju and Shan kept her company while she finished her meal. "You may call Anil and Rashi and tell them about my condition."

"I will call them tonight. Tomorrow morning my friend, Raman, is coming for a short visit," Raju said.

"Yes, I remember." She turned toward Shan and said, "Dr. Raman Jani is Raju's high school buddy. He has a busy medical practice in India." Shan was not in the mood to socialize, so he just nodded. The shades of worry had stolen his smile…Sumi dreaded the night alone but insisted that they go home and rest. Though Shan and Raju were not close, Sumi was glad that Raju was not alone that night.

The grim feelings dragged her down into a lonely corner, and all the forgotten pain and hurts surfaced. She had a hard time remembering. Was she ever happy? Sumi's mind was running in a circle. *No one tells the truth. This is the end of Sumi…What a way to go. Raju will have to find someone else. Oh! He will have difficulty fixing his own lunch tomorrow.* That simple thought made her cry.

When the nurse came in with her medicine, she wanted to scream at her. She wanted to scream at somebody, but she was too timorous to do that. She visualized her mother seated by her bedside with a worried look as she used to watch her for hours.

"No one bothered to stay with me." She found one more complaint.

It does not matter, why I hurt!
Everything that required healing,
has rushed to the surface appealing.
Tonight I want to hide in a burrow;
Somehow, I will face them tomorrow.

It seemed as though Sumi was being pulled into a dark tunnel, and she did not bother to look for a ray of hope. She simply succumbed to the gloom.

Sumi felt week and sick and eventually fell asleep.

The early morning nudging and poking by the nurse and technician woke her up. Sumi was numb. She was sure of the futility of the treatment. *I have seen my cousin slowly dying, leaving her small child behind. It is good that I don't have to face that misery,* she thought.

The sun got brighter, and she was left alone until the door opened, and two familiar eyes showed up behind a mask. Her eyes gave away the message, "Oh! I missed you," and his eyes replied, "I can't live without you."

"My friend Dr. Raman wanted to see you before he leaves," Raju said. His friend and Shan entered her room.

Sumi noticed that Shan and Raju seemed relaxed. Dr. Raman had helped them to understand Sumi's sickness and guided them to put it in the right perspective. He showed complete faith in the modern treatment, and he assured them that Sumi would be just fine. Sumi's mind wasn't ready to believe him, so she heard Dr. Raman's opinion as a window created for Raju and Shan to jump back into the flow of their activities and to leave her behind. She was quiet, so none of them could guess that her fragile mind was quivering with doubts.

Shan had to depart for India that evening. So with heavy hearts, they said good-bye. Raju told Sumi that he had to drop off Shan at the airport in the evening, but the following day, he had planned to spend several hours with her.

In the evening, Sumi was glad to see her friend Rashi, who took a few minutes to get adjusted in the mask and gown. Raju had briefly told her about Sumi's grave mood due to the serious nature of her illness. Rashi was worried for her friend, but in her cheerful voice, she said, "I see that my ever active friend is forced to rest for a while." Rashi made her smile.

"Yes, but these two days seemed long enough. I feel like running out of here. I want to go away from everyone." Rashi understood that she meant everyone except Raju. Rashi could see that every ounce of Sumi's being was screaming to get up and go to take care of her Raju. But her doubts were debilitating any of her positive thoughts of healing.

All this time Sumi was hiding her frustrations and fears from everyone, but Rashi had earned her trust. "I know that you are a friend with whom I can share my joys and sorrows, and our friendship can bear the weight of my grief," Sumi said.

She paused and looked into her friend's compassionate eyes. "Rashi, I do not want to be an obstacle in Raju's life. Will you and Anil see to it that Raju is all right after I am gone?"

Rashi was outraged. "And where do you think you are going?"

"I am not sure… You know! Raju gets so engrossed in his work and forgets to care for himself." She tried to change the subject.

"But Raju told me that you are going to be perfectly fine in no time." Rashi wasn't sure how to bring her out of the depression. "Okay, Can you do one thing? Just take this day as a gift and take a step forward," Rashi told Sumi.

Let's hold hands and ride through the storm.
Hold tight in case our hands slip and the
flow sways you off.
Pray, o my friend! With all your might,
and the cosmos will unite to make things
right.

Before Rashi left, she placed a get-well card on Sumi's nightstand. Sumi was tired and fell asleep.

She felt good after a short nap. She lazily read Rashi's handwritten card.

Dear Sumi,

I understand that you are overwhelmed, but if you don't take time to pull your wits together, the negative energy will suffocate your vitality. You have to pause and ask, "How am I going to handle this?" These were your exact words to me, remember?

I want to share a few lines I read in a good book. "You are put on this earth for some special mysterious reason, and when you are not enthusiastic about finding out what it is, you are betraying the mystery of the universe. This is nature's law. Before a dream is realized, the soul of the world tests everything you have learned along the way. As you go up the spiritual spiral staircase, the tests become harder. When the real test comes, that is the point most people give up..." Sumi, you are not one who gives up! So, my friend, I wish you courage and lots of love.

Rashi

Sumi straightened up in the bed and, for the first time, noticed the pink roses snuggled with white carnations in a shapely vase. She got up to add some water. She gently stroked the velvety petals and stared at Raju's and Shan's names on the tag. She felt calm and content thinking about Shan. She remembered the words he had said, "I cannot take away your grief, but our blessings will always be there to lessen it." She prayed for his safe journey to India.

The phone rang. Sumi was pleased to hear Shan's voice. "Raju and I are at the airport. I wanted to talk to you before I take off," Shan said.

"I wanted to talk to you too. I am going to be all right, really, I mean it…" Sumi said. When he heard that familiar determination in her voice, Shan's worries melted away in his tears.

The night slowly spread its veil. Sumi looked at the stars through the window and analyzed her thoughts. "Why do I not trust these doctors and my loved ones! My conscience is clouded with fear, and that's why there is no room for faith. I am trembling inside like a dry leaf. My Raju is standing there, unfolding his palms to give this quivering leaf a safe shelter. But I am adrift, ignoring his extended hands. Every step, easy or challenging, it is up to me how to take it. This sickness unfolds my understanding of the helplessness and fragility of life. If my illness lingers, I will have to face it.

"One thing I must not forget: death is inevitable. When it comes, gently put your body in its hands. No questions are asked of destiny. But until then, even if

I feel fear, I will move forward. I will open my heart and embrace every precious moment."

Raju had taken half a day off to sit and talk with Sumi. He was not sure how he would reconnect with Sumi, but his doubts vanished when he was received with a welcoming smile from Sumi. They talked about her feelings of the last several days, and he talked about his agony. His mask and gown were a constant reminder of the misery and uncertainty of their lives. Sumi's afternoon fever and coughing were still there.

"Shan will land in Mumbai in a couple of hours after almost twenty hours of travel! And then a few more hours to reach home," Raju said. They had decided that Shan would tell his family and then go to Vadodara to talk to Raju's parents about Sumi's sickness and recovery.

The silence made them forget everything but love. Raju lifted and covered Sumi's hand softly in both his hands like a precious keepsake. The words of their hearts, spoken through their fingers, sent waves of energy. Connection is the energy created when people feel that they are seen, heard, and valued; and that makes the flow of affection effortless.

On the tenth day, Sumi was out of isolation and was moved to share a room with another patient. The last days of her stay in the hospital were well spent in her creative writing with a new awakening. She was surprised by her new vision and understanding of some of life's troubling mysteries. She did not realize before the strength of love from far and near, the way she did in her sickness. She experienced the loving hearts beat very close; the physical distance does not matter much.

The day before her discharge from the hospital, she was floored with a bombshell order. In place of Dr. Tate, another old doctor came to her room and announced, "After this illness, it is routine that the patient has to check into a sanatorium for several months." Raju and Sumi were flabbergasted. Sumi's eyes stung with terrified tears.

"Dr. Tate never mentioned that. He is out of town, but somehow I will contact him," Raju said.

"It is your health. Do whatever you have to," the doctor said, and he walked out. Limitless questions ran through Sumi's mind while Raju went out to find out about Dr. Tate. He came back with good information. "Dr. Tate will be here tomorrow," he said.

Those long hours of distress…They both anxiously waited for the doctor. He came and explained the older doctor's traditional approach. Dr. Tate said, "The latest X-ray indicates the calcification of the infection in your lung. Sumi is safe to be with. As a precaution, Raju is on medication, and Sumi will continue to take these pills for one year…Now go and live a long and healthy life."

A second chance to live my life!
To breathe the air, to feel the rain!

A second chance to dare and dance!
To write the songs, to praise the Lord!

Sumi was feeling awkward entering her own home. Raju followed, carrying her bag. "Wow! You have kept the apartment so clean and neat," She was impressed.

"Yes, it is clean, but I cannot take the credit for it. Rashi had your key, so she must have done it," Raju said.

"You are right." Rashi walked in with a covered dish. "And here is your lunch. Taste it, and tell me what a good cook I am!"

Voice of Women

Bad things happen for mysterious reasons, and if a human accepts them as a petal of blessing from the universe, it turns out to be a new dawn after a dark night. In the darkness, one is vulnerable to danger but can be vulnerable to divine revelation too. Some of the richest treasures can be found in the dark.

Several months before, Sumi got the entry into the magical world of California with Raju. He moved on through the door to the other side, but Sumi found herself confused, staring at the closed door. She kept on struggling to do things she thought she was supposed to do. And then she got sick and got lost in a bottomless tunnel. The darkness of her sickness gave her three weeks to clear her vision—a blessing in disguise.

That day, she was reentering the magical world as a new person, one who can see the light beyond the open door…

Sumi had talked with Raju about what she had planned to do after she came home. She asked Rashi, who worked in the admissions office, about registration and the beginning of classes. Sumi wanted to register for a new subject: Introduction to Computers. In the early seventies, the computer courses were considered essential for future jobs. The big machines and rolling wheels were very fascinating. And the second course was in her field of study. Classes started, and she was among a different group of people, and in a way, it was a relief to her.

Sumi needed some time to reconnect with her old self. The youthful circle on the campus proved to be the best remedy. Rejuvenated, Sumi was excited being a student again. She loved the challenging subjects and enjoyed the company of other students.

Every Friday, Rashi and Sumi planned to have a group lunch at the campus cafeteria. Brilliant, confident, and also some struggling, lonely women met them at lunch time. Slowly, the group became larger with white, black, and brown faces.

One thing led to another, and there was an initiation of an organization they called Voice of Women. The organization, backed by the university, managed to get a hotline and began to assist foreign female students. The organization did not have many rules or restrictions. Simple requests for help would come in, and they were happy to provide guidance…But one day, when Sumi was taking calls, she heard a meek voice on the line.

"Hi, I don't know whom to call, but my husband is hurting me. He has stepped out for a few minutes, so I called." Sumi was taken aback. She knew that she had to be quick to reply.

"Can you come to our office?" Sumi said. The woman agreed to come after one hour, as soon as her husband went to work. Sumi was very nervous. She immediately called Rashi.

That lady happened to be the wife of an accountant at the university. They had recently moved to the USA from India. The wife worked in the cafeteria, so she had seen and heard Sumi and Rashi talking with other ladies. Her English was very poor. Away from her family, she was at the mercy of her controlling, abusive husband. Sumi and Rashi had to prepare a new set of rules quickly. They contacted domestic violence organizations in the city and put some resources to work.

Sumi gave this victim's case name Dina. They secretly met the victim, sometimes Rashi and Sumi both or Sumi alone. Dina was not allowed by her husband to learn English or drive. She had to beg for every penny from her husband. Any little mistake would end up in a sharp beating, and then she was ordered to hide the wounds by wearing long-sleeved clothes. His threat to her was, "If you will open your mouth, I will send you back to India, and no one will let you put your foot in the door. You worthless, stupid woman!"

Dina was advised to move to a women's shelter, but she did not want to leave her home. Sumi took her to a pro bono lawyer, who said, "You can rightfully live at home, and if your husband tries to push you out, call the police." When the layers of ignorance were removed, the inner energy shined. Dina was cautious but no longer scared, mute, or submissive. The victim learned, "One definition of 'fearless' is to be alert and aware of the danger. The controlling cowards are afraid of the resistance."

Her husband had to go to India for two weeks, so Rashi and Sumi discussed some strategies with Dina.

Sumi was finished with her classes but was getting more involved with the volunteer group. A small room on the campus was assigned to their organization. She had posted a big poster of Swami Vivekananda in the room, which said, "Even the least work done for others awakens the power within. Even thinking the least good of others gradually instills into a heart the strength of a lion." Swami Vivekananda was a well-known spiritual giant of India who became famous for his representation of Hinduism at the Parliament of Religions held in Chicago in 1893.

That evening, Sumi was on her way to the library. She walked under the canopy of green leaves and the glorious deep purple blooms of the crape myrtles. The hazy, hushed evening made her uneasy, and she quickened her steps.

Sumi was tickled to hear: "I see that Miss Sumi is in a big hurry to meet her date—TGIF," Rashi came out from her office building. She knew that, lately, Sumi and Raju had started every Friday a date-night routine. Sumi would go and wait for Raju at the library.

"I am so glad to see you. It is only six o'clock, and already, it is so dark and creepy," Sumi said.

"Sumi, I was passing by the cafeteria, and I saw Dina talking to a tall, husky guy who could be her husband!" Rashi spoke in serious tone.

"Oh! Really? I hope he is not creating more problems for her." Sumi was concerned about Dina.

Sumi entered the library and went upstairs. She had about half an hour to wait. She put her purse down on a corner table and went to the far corner to look for a poetry book. She was engrossed in the treasured volumes. All of a sudden, someone forcefully pushed her into a corner and stood resting his long arms on the wall over her head.

Sumi lost her voice in fear. She looked up and saw an angry face. "You good-for-nothing, nosy woman! Stay away from my wife. I am warning you. Do *not* butt into my life, or else…" He just wheezed.

Sumi got her courage back. She raised her voice. "Or else what? Get away from me this instant! You do not scare me." Sumi tried to push him away, but he was planted securely.

Raju arrived and saw Sumi's purse on the table— but no Sumi. Next, he heard her shouting voice, and he ran to the end of the hall. In the far corner, he saw the back of a man. "Who is there?" Raju shouted.

The man ran in the other direction toward a small staircase and disappeared.

She stopped Raju from chasing the man. "I am sure he is Dina's husband." Sumi was shaken, but she brushed it off. Raju was more disturbed than her and tried his best to spend their evening as they had planned.

The experience was a shocking revelation for Sumi. Her efforts to help Dina were intensified. Dina decided to end her marriage. As a domestic violence victim, she was entitled to a special visa to stay in the USA, and her husband was deported.

After that case, more victims came forward and the Voice of Women branched out in a different direction. Most victims were Asians who were financially and socially dependent on their spouses. Sumi encouraged the victims to take control of their lives and move forward.

> If you be like a rock and cling to be secure,
> you will slip and fall;
> because the world is like quicksand.
> In the ever-changing life, you be like a river,
> graciously go and flow forever.

Sumi started communicating with other organizations in the USA and India. The volunteer activity consumed her time and her thoughts. But still many times she wondered, *How in the world did I get into this?*

Smiling Dawn

Sumi was in her cozy bed, singing with the angels in her dream. Suddenly, the midnight thunder and lightning woke her up. The frightened Sumi turned around and tried to hide in Raju's arms...He smiled and embraced the alarmed intruder. After that, she was too distracted to hear any rumble of thunder. The cloud and night rained in romantic harmony.

After the wonderful rain, the revitalized nature was invigorating for the young lovers. In the blissful morning, Raju and Sumi walked hand in hand through nature's creation, a perfect magic land. The weeping willow trees were welcoming the early walkers and joggers gracefully, with their sweeping branches forming the familiar falling canopy.

> The humming birds were
> kissing the convivial flowers.
> The sun removed the clouds to see
> the unsullied bride.
> And that's the way the smiling dawn
> looked at the earth.

"I can't believe that Shan's baby girl will be three weeks old tomorrow. Traditionally, the father's sister gives name to the child, so I am thinking to suggest the name Amy. Raju, what do you think? Do you like it?" Sumi said.

Raju was in a trance with nature, and so he took several moments to reply. Happily, he said, "Oh! Yes. I love it." Lately, he had managed to find these relaxing minutes from his hectic schedule.

Two weeks before, he had suffered a major setback in his research work. He was very disappointed and felt that he would never be able to prove his theory.

Sumi had to encourage and help him to recharge and reevaluate his steps. "What brings success to a man? Failures, followed by tenacity and enthusiasm, and you have an added bonus—me," she had said. "Many of us have faith in you, and I know that you will not let us down." Raju recognized his irrational intensity and saw the need for relaxation. He included a yoga class and the long walks with Sumi in his daily activities. Sometimes, it becomes necessary to take one step back to maintain equilibrium.

Sumi took her last pill of the year and went for a checkup. She nervously sat in the doctor's office, holding Raju's hand. She told Raju that she would not be able to bear any more bad news.

Dr. Tate entered his office, holding Sumi's lab result. He stopped and said, "Wow! I have to give you an update about your health and one surprise."

The tone of his voice gave Sumi some confidence. "Sumi is perfectly all right. The surprise *is*…you are pregnant!" the doctor continued. Raju and Sumi fell into each other's arms, forgetting about the world around them.

As soon as they got home, the first phone call was made to Raju's parents and then to her parents. Shan had gotten a new phone line in their house, so they did not have to run to the neighbor's house anymore.

The news of the baby changed the whole dynamic of their lives. Sumi's life started breathing at a different pace. The feelings of all-embracing and all-inclusive love enveloped her. The dreams and plans began to unfold like the flowers in the spring. Sumi felt that she was sitting at the edge of a mischievously rushing river and getting cool splashes of water on her face. She did not know whether to walk, run, or fly to be with her beloved friends and family in India. She wanted to share the joy of anticipation and uncertainty. She was missing Priya the most. But she had accepted the reality that Raju's work would keep them in the wonderland of California for some time. And she was perfectly happy to be there.

> There are countless flowers in the garden of
> God.
> I would feel incomplete without a flower of
> my own.
> I hold the seed of our love in my womb,
> as the celestial strings intone a song.

Sumi took one more course at the university to strengthen her knowledge, which could be helpful in securing a job in her field in the future. As the months went on, they had many discussions about their future plans. Sumi wanted to go back and settle in India as soon as Raju's project could be completed and his bond with the university was over. He was not objecting, but it was hard for him to decide. He would not leave his research work without achieving the anticipated result.

Raju's parents arrived at the delivery time to help. The same afternoon, Raju's mother informed that Ajay had secured a job with an international company.

"The news is—Ajay exchanged a promise ring with Komal the day before we left India," Raju's mom said.

Raju was shocked. "What! With Komal?" Sumi gave him a quizzical look. Then he paused, took a deep breath, and said, "He must be lured in by her fashionable look." Before Raju say anything more, his father handed him Ajay's letter. The letter said,

Dearest brother and bhabhi,

I know you will be surprised to hear about Komal and me. Komal, a fashionable and shallow girl, whom I knew as a spoiled daughter of a rich dishonest businessman...But destiny kept us throwing in front of each other. We have

*been working together for the same
company since last one year.
Bhai! She is good to the core. She has
moved away from her dishonest family
and declared an open protest against his
corrupted father. She is exciting, enticing,
and challenging. We are crazy about each
other...I love you both. Wish you all the
best for my niece or nephew!*

Namaste,

Ajay

Raju laughed and said, "Well, looks like they will make a good pair, a crazy boy and a rebellious girl."

The time had come—the epic of emotions. They entered the hospital worried and happy, with unique palpitation. Rashi and other friends were buzzing around, bubbling with excitement and joy. Raju chose to wait outside the delivery room. With the nurse's signal, he rushed in, followed by his parents...Sumi's face was shining like the moon as she announced, "It's a boy!" Raju held his son and let the tears of joy flow blatantly.

"A birth happens maybe every second in this world. Still every single time, it is a miracle," Grandpa Sam said. They named their son Ravi—the sun.

The first few days, she enjoyed the help and attention. Only after bringing him home did Sumi realize how much time and attention a little person needed. After two months, her parents-in-law were to return to India, leaving Sumi alone to care for the baby and the household. Raju admitted that he could not allot much time to stay home. The fact that he seemed to have a one-track mind, totally focused on his work, was something Sumi respected; but she also felt annoyed because nothing else mattered to him when he was working.

Among all these commotions, she got an offer from a lecturer friend at the University of Vadodara. That friend needed a replacement for a semester, and she wanted to recommend Dr. Suman Mody. Everyone was impressed by this offer for Sumi.

After some discussion, Sumi decided with a heavy heart that she would go to India. Raju also felt that Sumi and the baby would be more comfortable with two families in India.

Sumi's volunteer work was recognized by the university, and she made certain that it was running well before she left. When she told Rashi about her plan to go back to India, Rashi was very upset and could not speak with Sumi for the entire day. She talked it out with Anil in the evening, and after that, they both came to spend some time with the Modys.

"Rashi, we are friends forever. We have met in this lifetime once, and we will meet again. We are only a phone call away. Don't be so sad, my friend. This makes very hard for me to depart," Sumi assured her.

Before leaving, Sumi told Raju, "I will not put any pressure on you. You may take as long as you need to reach your goal." She looked at their precious child and said, "We will be waiting for you. I will learn to live without you, but promise me that it will not be for too long."

At dawn, I recite the verse of love in his
ears,
and he embraces me longingly.
I am edgy and fearful, but he is quiet and
patient.
His gentleness soothes my restlessness.
Sadly...like a song of waves, I drift away.

So Sumi went back to India with her in-laws and her precious son, Ravi. Raju's parents were immensely thankful for the joy of taking their daughter-in-law and grandson home.

The new relationship evolves on four pillars: what one says and how another perceives, how the action–reaction cycle is handled and how much both parties value the relationship.

Here She Belongs

The airplane was flying in the blue sky. The giant man-made bird took a dive through the cave of the clouds. It was scary but exhilarating when it touched the ground. Sumi had returned to her motherland. The early morning flight brought them to Vadodara from Mumbai. Ajay, Nina, and Auntie were eagerly waiting to see the baby. Once they were home, Sumi hardly had to worry about Ravi. This baby would be nurtured with love and care in the joint family, like a tune carried uninterrupted by a group of singers.

Sumi rested for several hours at her in-laws' home. She came out and saw some kites flying around. It gave her nostalgic feelings about her mom's home. She felt like a kite held by the thread, tugging at her heart. She wished to be in the bosom of her family. Her mind gave her a nudge, and she responded, "Yes, I know, this is my family too."

Sumi's parents were informed of their safe arrival, and Ajay would bring Sumi and Ravi to their house on Saturday by car. Sumi was sure that her mother would exclaim, "Oh, after four days!"

The second day at noontime, Sumi was setting the table for lunch. The doorbell rang, and intuitively, a thought flickered, *It must be my mom.* And there she was! Mother and daughter embraced each other; the joyful vibrations resonated…The sorrow of their separation gave in, and their eyes flooded with tender tears. Januma gave her a gentle kiss.

Sumi's mother-in-law rushed out of the kitchen, and her father-in-law walked in from the patio, holding their grandson. They warmly welcomed Januma and handed her the bundle of joy. Ravi's innocent smile reflected on all the adoring faces…

As soon as they were alone, Januma inquired about Sumi's health. She said, "Since I heard about your sickness, my eyes have not been dry any day. My heart was stuck in my throat. Only I know how I have endured these past months. Now when I see you look like a pink rose, I will now be able to have some peace." That night, Sumi wrote to Raju in her letter:

Mom's heart fluttered and fled to be here.
The tears were rolling, not aware they were
flowing.
In wordless whispers,
she conveyed us her blessings.

Ajay came home with his fiancée, Komal. She was quite different compared to Sumi. It was intriguing the way Komal was dressed in the skimpy clothes and strange jewelry. She approached everyone very casually, except Ravi. She was crazy about the baby, whom she carried and cuddled the whole time she was there.

The trio was in the patio, so Sumi brought out a blanket for the baby.

Sumi was almost out of the door when she heard Komal whisper, "Ajay, even with the baby fat, your bhabhi is so beautiful."

Sumi turned and jokingly said, "I heard that!" In return, Komal gave an unbridled laugh. It was a bit strange, but that amused Ajay and Sumi too.

After three years, Sumi was returning to her childhood home. Just the thought of meeting her youth again as a grown woman with her baby made her wistful. When they pulled into the front of the house, at least a dozen people rushed out of the house to the gate behind Shan. Her brother came near the car as if he did not see anyone else but his sister. Shan helped Sumi out of the car and hugged her like never before, because he had seen her near death the last time in California.

Sona made her way through the crowd. Mamu was standing there, smiling next to her father. Sumi touched her father's feet and then did pranam to her mamu. Sumi was lost amongst other relatives, while Ravi was transported into a cozy baby hammock, a ghodiyu.

She was immersed in the genuine lagoon of approval, admiration, and affection of her relatives. Her parents and mamu looked much older with some added wrinkles. A sorrowful thought touched her soul, reminding her of what she had missed in the past few years. Sumi promised herself never to take this down-to-earth love for granted.

She had yet to meet her niece, Amy, who was napping. As usual, Ajay and Shan were sharing many funny stories with the family. The two-year-old groggily walked into the living room on her unsteady feet and stopped as soon as she saw an unfamiliar face and a baby! Her wide eyes found her mom and ran to her. Sona held her and introduced her to Sumifoi and cousin Ravi. Sumi was immediately smitten with Amy and wanted to hold, hug, and kiss her. But the little one would not come near her. Well, it took some coaxing and a few chocolates from Sumi—and finally, the princess Amy came into her aunt's arms, and her Sumifoi showered her with affection.

The next day, when Priya arrived to meet Sumi, their reunion reminded people of a noisy orchestra. Priya's two children along with the other two in the house were singing in a chorus at times. Januma's house was filled with delightful noise.

One peaceful day, Sumi was sitting in the backyard. Januma came and sat next to her and uneasily asked, "Sumi! How was your life in America? How come you returned alone? Are you and Raju getting along okay?" When she received an enthusiastic, positive response from Sumi, she relaxed.

"One more question. When you were sick, how did he treat you? The true identity of your spouse is revealed when you are in deep trouble or seriously ill," Januma said.

"Ma, he did not waiver for a single minute. When I thought I was going to die, I turned away from him. But very patiently, he stood by me and pulled me out of the depression." Her emotional voice touched Januma's soul and moistened her eyes.

Early in the morning, Shan announced to Sumi, "You be ready for some surprises. I am warning you so you won't have a heart attack. Okay?"

"I know Sunday evening you have planned a party here…There goes your surprise," cleverly Sumi said. Shan walked away, grinning. Sunday evening, Sumi wrapped herself in a beautiful sari and welcomed her relatives with her prince in her arms. The people who had missed seeing her at her sudden, secret wedding satisfied their curiosity by staring at her.

She went to put Ravi down in the cradle. Right then, someone came quietly behind her and covered her eyes and spoke in a disguised voice, "Tell me, tell me, who am I?"

"Anu? I don't believe this," Sumi screamed.

"You better believe it," another voice said. Her cousin Risa followed with Priya. The screaming and hugging went on.

Shan came and said, "Oh, crazy girls! Calm down. Let me make sure that Sumi is not fainting. Sona, take her pulse."

Sumi dramatically leaned on Sona. "Yes. Hold me. I am overpowered by the spell of delight!" The miles of distance or the long time-lapse did not matter in the circle of friends. They were talking to each other as if they were continuing a conversation from yesterday.

Late in the night, all the ladies gathered on the terrace, while the children and men succumbed to slumber. Sumi thought she must be the luckiest person in the world for having such good friends.

I feel so rich and full of mischief,
No mask, no pretense, and no prerequisite.
The simple merriment tags
among the circle of friends.

Ajay went back on Sunday afternoon. Sumi and Ravi were to stay with her parents for at least three months. Then Sumi had to go back to prepare for her teaching assignment in Vadodara. Raju called one time, but she knew how expensive it would be, so she kept it short.

Sumi began to hear the subliminal complaints from her mother about her daughter-in-law. Fortunately, they were not serious, and Januma, a wise mom-in-law, had her sense of priorities straight.

Sumi's father had been somewhat aloof and a loner in the household managed by the younger generation. Once in a while, upset, Januma would go to his room and grumble. So when Sumi was around, her mom shared some stories with her. Then Sumi would hear the same episodes from Sona's perspective. Sumi clearly saw the different sides of human nature and remained a compassionate listener for both of them without taking anyone's side. She wanted to be a confidant to her mother and a lifelong friend for Sona.

The children were the center of attention and attraction. That day, Sumi witnessed pure innocent delight. Shan was chasing Amy, and the family clapped and encouraged her to run. Amy would run and would pause intermittently to kiss her grandparents, her mom, and Sumi. Ravi was jumping in Sumi's lap. Sumi said to Sona, "It seems children think they are entertaining us, and we think we are playing for them."

> Who is chasing whom? A simple silly race,
> Childhood runs to us, gathers in embrace.
> Sparkling shiny smile a blissful resonance,
> Darling little ones hold divine innocence.

She felt content and happy to spend time with her family.

Sumi returned to Vadodara and got busy with her work plans. The night before her first class, she reread Raju's encouraging letter. She felt his presence accompany her all the way to the classroom.

She was dressed in a white-and-pink sari. Before she stepped out, her mother-in-law said, "Beta, wait!" She put a spoonful of sweet curd, a symbol of good luck, in Sumi's mouth.

Sumi picked up Ravi and hugged and kissed him and whispered, "Mama will be back soon. Love you, bye."

Ravi pulled out, "Tata," from his short vocabulary, which his uncle had taught. With exclamation of wonder, he clasped his hands when everyone laughed. Delighted, Sumi hugged her sweet love, bursting with life energy, one more time. He was pulling away to look at the running toy train, so Sumi had to put him down. She bid pranam to her Ammi and Papa and warmheartedly proceeded to face the tough world.

She was thankful that she was familiar with the university campus as a student, but as a teacher, it seemed like a different world. She came across many familiar faces in the staff room. The history unraveled, some good and some not so good. But she was totally focused on her job. She knew that this opportunity could be the most important feather in her career's crown.

Sumi was amazed by Raju's followers at the university. The professors and graduate students had all the current information about his research work through his published papers. She was often asked about his latest progress and when would he come back. Sumi had been struggling with the same unanswered question, when will he come back? In his last letter, he had said, "Most days, I am so engrossed in my work that I forget to stop...But don't panic. I usually leave as soon as Anil or Rashi calls and orders me to go home to rest."

She was delighted whenever she was introduced as Dr. Suman Mody—Dr. Raju's wife. The semester was almost over. Sumi had been in India for ten months, away from Raju. The melancholy of separation was getting too intense for them.

Where are you, my love!
I want to put my head on your shoulder and
cry.
I wish to look in your eyes and smile.
These precious moments on the wings of
time,
fly away from my lonely heart.

It was a misty evening. She was lost in the memories with the sway of the swing. All of a sudden, she heard Ajay's voice. "Bhabhi! Come and look who is here!"

She rushed out but stopped at the sight of the individual. Sumi's heart skipped a beat. "Oh! Nick! I am surprised to see you...after a long time!" she said.

"Yes, it has been a very long time," Nick replied calmly. They both seemed nervous.

After some casual conversation, Ajay said, "I have to pick up Komal, but we will be back very soon." Her parents-in-law had gone for a stroll with Ravi.

Nick and Sumi talked with deep emotions like two loyal friends. In the quiet of the evening, they shared the ups and downs of their lives. In the back of Sumi's mind, one question was popping up, *What if I had accepted his proposal of marriage?* And the answer was clear. *No, it was not meant to be...* She was glad to have him as a friend.

Sumi's parents-in-law came back with Ravi from their stroll and invited Nick to stay for supper. And he readily accepted.

When the past meets present,
A cloud, a thunder, and then the sprinkle of rain.
Whatever happened, it was for a reason.
We have to abide the wind of each season.

Out of the blue, one day, the excited voice of Raju announced on the speakerphone in the Mody household in Vadodara, "Ma and Papa! With your blessings, I have done it. The result of my research has been proven to be correct. It has generated a big hubbub on an international level. Hey, Ajay, are you listening? This is your famous brother speaking." And a jovial response was unanimous.

"Is Sumi there?" Raju asked. The family dispersed as she picked up the phone. Raju was bubbling with the love lyrics, and she responded playfully, "Me too," with her soft laugh. After the call, Sumi went in her room and poured out her love and joy on a pink paper and mailed the letter to Raju.

The days and months passed by, and the trial waiting game was still on. Raju was wrapping up in California, and some job offers were under consideration. But the biggest conflict for him was whether to continue in the USA or to go back to their homeland. The separation from Sumi and Ravi was compelling him to make a right decision soon.

Sumi had gotten involved with different projects in Vadodara. The university had organized a symposium at a venue—about an hour drive from the city. Sumi was on the committee and was an overnight guest at the hotel. The two-day program was attended by many professionals from all over India. In the huge auditorium, Sumi was welcoming the guests onto the stage. From the corner of her eye, she noticed the familiar face of Minu in the audience, who waved at her. But Sumi chose not to wave back.

Knowing Minu, she was not going to leave her alone. At the lunch break, Sumi was chatting with the last guest. Minu came and pulled up an empty chair and sat down. Sumi said good-bye to the guest and turned toward Minu.

"Hi, Minu, how are you?" Sumi asked, but her mind was mumbling, *What are you up to now? Whose life are you trying to mess up?*

"I am okay. I know you do not have time or desire to talk to me. I will come to the point. I am sorry for the troubles I caused you. I apologize. I have learned my lesson. I am divorced and miserable," Minu said.

"Oh! That is sad. You will be okay." It did not take long for Minu to soften up Sumi. But this time, Sumi was keenly aware of what she was capable of. Sumi remained friendly with her, because that was who she was—a caring person.

> The likes and dislikes, adoration and
> abhorrence
> will eventually end with an intuitive response.
> The betrayal would heal with
> the passion of compassion.
> Forgive and forget, move on to the circle of
> elation.

It was the last hour of the seminar. Sumi was speaking about the empowerment of women in the field of science, as well as the home front. The elite group of scholars was attentively listening to her. Sumi concluded with the essence of the seminar.

"Has the day come when beauty and knowledge, ingenuity and virtue, the weakness of body and strength of her soul have been united in a woman? The opportunities we have to create and promote will not be handed down to us. The family life and motherhood provide access to our true essence and will also give a woman insight into the mirror of correlation, because all relationships are a reflection of our inner harmony…" Sumi stopped for a moment when she heard the coos of her child but considered the sound as a delusion and continued.

"As my mother says, 'The key to any woman's success is the synergistic energy.' So let's make our family a source of strength, the men our allies, and our children our inspiration. When we harness the forces of patience, acceptance, and awareness, the attainment of good fortune follows with a graceful ease."

She finished her speech. Before the applause ended, the chairperson got up and said, "Thank you, Dr. Suman. I was just informed that we have a renowned scientist in the audience, our own Dr Raju Mody. Please come to the stage."

All heads turned to the far end of the auditorium. No one was more surprised than Sumi. Raju hesitantly walked to the stage, holding a gleeful Ravi. Sumi's sparkling eyes and delighted smile welcomed Raju. She took her son in her arms. The whole scenario was so natural and unique. The audience was mesmerized…

Upon the request, Raju had to take the microphone. He said, "Greetings. I apologize for barging in your assembly. I landed in Vadodara this morning and couldn't wait to surprise my wife, so I had to follow her here. Please carry on your good work."

The pearl of this memorable moment was added in the chain of their story line. On the way home, Raju told Sumi that he had decided to accept an offer